I0456892

the prodigal

Also from *what tradition books*:

The Whores of Coxcomb Hall by Egg Taylor

The Ghost of Neil Diamond by David Milnes

All hail *The Ghost of Neil Diamond*:

"The Ghost of Neil Diamond is the best novel I've read in years . . . Storytelling, architecture, painting and poetry - a few rare novels excel in all four categories. The Ghost of Neil Diamond is one such book. Ghost is a beautiful cathedral - at the risk of sounding effusive you should make a pilgrimage. It's that superb . . ."

dissidentbooks.com   New York

"We have a real corker of a tale on our hands . . . It's a special find - a story with a uniqueness that makes you wonder what else the author has up his sleeve . . . a thoroughly enjoyable and idiosyncratic story that holds your attention until the rather brilliant end."

bookmunch.co.uk   Manchester UK

"This is a work of unexpected substance. . . a dark comedy stemming from the howling despair of a man who is out of his element in every way . . . a book that subtly plays with the tropes associated with its subject matter to raise some interesting questions about what represents the real, and what constitutes the fake"

harmlessfraud.com   Dublin Ireland

"A rare find, a totally original and fascinating novel that holds your interest from beginning to end. I highly recommend The Ghost of Neil Diamond if you're tired of reading the same old shit and want to check out something truly unique."

alternativereel.com   Florida

the prodigal

david milnes

what tradition books

www.whattradition.com

Chapter One

Please Call Ebbages

Claremont Villas
Lonsdale Road
Notting Hill Gate
London W 11
Thurs 4th Nov '77

Dear Anna,

This must seem odd. He finally takes the trouble to put pen to paper and now you have an opportunity to gloat. I swore that would never happen. For once I was to be truly resolute. I know, I know.

There have been many times over the last few months when I have desperately wanted to come home, to chuck it all in. (Chuck what in? I hear you asking.) Times when the sheer physical discomfort seemed just too much. Faintness of heart, lack of grit - call it what you will. But during these bleak spells I always knew it was not enough to turn tail on account of circumstances alone. It would have done little good to arrive back on my doorstep feeling as awful as when I left it. I could only come back when I felt in my heart of hearts ready to come back.

I shall not bore you with the history of my days here. There were a few nights sleeping out, I'm afraid; then a ghastly hostel in Paddington . . . It's not so bad now, though. Tolerably comfortable.

Survival focuses the mind. Oh yes it does, my dear.

I want you to know, completely and without doubt, that I fully forgive you your closeness where money was concerned. You had to protect yourself. Of course you did. I could have wrecked everything. And it was as well that I set out naked and alone, with nothing, no hidden crutch. But please forgive me the things I said at that time. I was desperate. My last throw of the die, if you like. Caution to the winds. The idle winds.

To discover one's whole life has been a lie, a waste, a folly, a wilful delusion - this is a terrible thing. Though I have done my utmost, throughout, to keep

Well, I can't finish that.

The fact is I am over the worst, I'm sure now, and I shall be coming home as soon as possible. If those words bring a modicum of joy to your heart, Anna, perhaps there is a chance of happiness for us yet.

We shall return to our original plans. Please call Ebbages. Put the house in their hands directly. I have no desire whatever to remain in Ipswich - or indeed this country! - a moment longer than absolutely necessary. We'll rent in Manosque until our affairs are settled. I don't mind going West a bit, even to Uzes, if that's what you want. I am in a mood to compromise. And to listen.

The move and the travelling will be wretched but once it's over . . .

I look forward to your reply by return. Please. I shan't go back over what I have written. It would be wrong to strive for the exact phrase. Such artifice. I do very much look forward to seeing you again, my dear.

Your loving husband,

Gerry

Chapter Two

A Free Lunch

Gerry had never been a pub person. He knew nothing about Fullers, Watneys or Tetleys, and he had never even heard of all these continental lagers that now slaked the nation's thirst for oblivion. Holsten Pils, indeed. What on earth was that? It flowed from a gold and yellow lozenge embossed with a coat of arms. Gerry sighed and his gaze drifted behind the bar to the wine cabinet, next to a grubby serving hatch. All the wines were bad, though. Very, very bad. Hungarian, Bulgarian and so on. Make Time for Wine, said a slightly squiffy sticker on the cabinet glass.

"I'm buying lunch and all accompanying beverage, Gerald," opened his host. "So what's your poison?"

Gerry had no idea what he wanted.

"I'll have whatever you're having, if you'd be so kind."

His host tried to catch the attention of the barman, a plump, flushed, fortyish fellow in a greasy blue suit, who was wrestling with a packet of Pork Scratchings.

Pink jowls, pink gins, Gerry silently observed.

"Er, two pints of Fullers, Mr Barman!" Gerry's host declared. "And two Today's Specials!"

On the words 'two Today's Specials!' the packet of Pork Scratchings exploded. Rinds were scattered all over the bar and all over the filthy carpet. The barman stood still, staring down at the mess he'd made.

"Fuck'em one an' all!"

Oh dear, Gerry thought. What profane wretch art thou?

The barman chose the largest scratching from the bar and popped it in his mouth. He dusted his hands and set to work. All this without a look, let alone a good afternoon, to his solitary customers. He scribbled the Today's Specials on a slip and stuffed the slip into a hand already waiting on the serving hatch.

Gerry noted that attendant hand: a female hand, careworn, palm up and open, pale and lifeless, as if severed there on the block of the hatch.

Well, one could think of better places for a free lunch, for goodness' sake.

More silence as the pints were drawn.

"A pleasing brew, I think you'll find," said his host, sliding the first across.

It was a remark that caused Gerry to frown faintly at the mug of muddy beer now in front of him. He'd been only too willing to take up the invitation of his surprise visitor, this well-spoken stranger with the educated and confident air, but now certain expressions, harmless clichés, taken together, had begun to grate, to breed suspicion.

He was led by his host from the bar to a corner seat by the window. Gerry glanced about as he followed, stooping with the weight of his pint mug. They were absolutely the only souls in the place, on a Friday lunch time.

Before sitting down his host stopped and took his first

sip of beer.

"Cheers!"

Gerry stopped too, straightened and sipped in reply.

"Cheers."

His host sat, unbuttoned his greatcoat, and relaxed into his cushioned corner seat. He spread himself out as if this was where he always sat in this saloon bar, as if this was his cosy corner in his local pub.

"I'm sure we'll come to an amicable agreement, Gerry. You're a fair-minded chap, if you don't mind me being old-fashioned."

You rather like being old-fashioned, don't you, if you don't mind me being something or other, Gerry wanted to reply, as he pulled out his chair. But he didn't say that or anything like it. He sat down carefully with his full mug of beer.

"Given that I'll be quitting the place very soon – possibly tomorrow, or Sunday – I don't much care what you do. It's a ghastly hole and you're welcome to it. I'm expecting a letter tomorrow morning which will confirm the decision."

Then Gerry lowered his head and squared his mug on its beer mat, trying to tidy up what he'd just said. He'd already made one mistake about this young man. Beneath the coat was a dark jumper covering a plain white shirt. The collar of the shirt was over-starched and fastened at the neck button, but there was no tie. The coat had been done up to the very top so it rode over the front of the shirt collar, and Gerry had wrongly taken his host to be a man of the cloth.

Gerry's suspicions deepened as his host removed his spectacles and began cleaning them with a linen handkerchief. A pressed linen handkerchief. And now a gentle frown, thoughtful, concerned, accompanied the cleaning of the lenses: his host was about to broach a matter of some importance.

"So come on, Gerry - " holding a lens to the light – "What's the story? Out with it! A man of your age - and your accomplishment - shouldn't be shacked up in dear old Claremont Villas, should he?"

Gerry had been used to meaningless flattery all his life, heaps of it, cartloads of it, but there was a strain of condescension in this young man's manner that was entirely unfamiliar to him. Very original, and very brazen indeed. Quite unforgivable. A voice told him to abandon the free lunch here and now, to go home and hide away in his dark, cold rooms. But another, stronger voice, begged to seize this chance to talk and talk and talk, even to a perfect stranger, even if it didn't do any good.

At this juncture the barman arrived with the Today's Specials. Such service! The meal was a steak and kidney pie fresh from the hot shelf and still in its foil dish. There was a low mound of crinkle chips on the side. The free lunch looked rather sorry for itself, Gerry considered. Accompanying sauces and condiments were set between their plates in a lidless tupperware container.

"Ah, great. Thanks awfully," his host quacked to the surly barman, who, as he turned to retreat, actually farted softly, as if by way of reply.

Gerry scowled. Good grief.

"Steak and kidney pie, Gerry!" His host picked up his knife and fork and tucked in straightaway. "Bon appétit!"

At the other side of the table Gerry split the pastry of his pie. The gravy rushed out with a noisome, dogmeat stench, enriched by the barman's fart. He put down his cutlery and drank some more beer. It was foul. He put the mug down too, noisily. This was a ghastly lunch. Yet across the table his host was stuffing it away, lapping it up. His full lips were glossy with gravy and he was already halfway through his pie. He stopped eating and took a long drink, leaving sizeable flakes of pastry on the surface of his beer.

"So the kids gave you a hard time, Gerry," his host prompted between mouthfuls, still keen to get a conversation started. "I wonder what such toughies would have made of my own alma mater. I was at Gordonstoun, you know. With Charleyboy, as a matter of fact . . ."

Out of some old world courtesy Gerry began to eat the food, and this depressed effort of will absorbed all his concentration. These days he kept remembering, with increasing bitterness, his headmaster's farewell speech, in which he was repeatedly and affectionately described as "a deeply civilized man". He came across a lump of gristle, pale and shiny under the gravy, which even his manners ("Please raise your glasses, Ladies and Gentlemen - I give you Gerry! To Gerry, everyone! - Come on! – Come on, there! - A deeply civilized man!") could not make him fork and bring to his mouth. He toyed with it, nudging it under one flap of pastry and another, until he found a roomy corner for it. He tried a few of the crinkle chips, which were tepid on the outside and cool on the inside, then decided that he'd done his best and set his knife and fork together in the middle of the plate, like a good boy. He went back to the dark beer.

"Contemporanus with Prince Hal himself!"

Gerry set down his beer mug without drinking. What was going on here? How speedily this episode had soured. Revulsion and impatience quickened to anger. What was he doing in this rotten, rotten English pub, eating its repulsive food, drinking its disgusting beer, with this overgrown public school boy? What was he doing?

"Excuse me." He got fussily to his feet and stood behind his chair. He gripped the back of the chair with both hands and cocked his learned head. "I'm afraid I must go home. Not feeling too well."

His host stared up open-mouthed. "Oh! . . . That's too bad, Gerald."

"If you'd care to call again some other time, we can discuss your proposal in more detail, perhaps, if I'm still there. And if I'm up to it."

"What?"

His host wiped the corners of his mouth with his linen handkerchief. He tried to compose himself, resting his arm along the back of the corner seat, his handkerchief dangling from his fingers, soiled with gravy.

"I thought it was all settled, Gerald."

"No it isn't." Gerry's words were clipped. He was up to this. If a confrontation were called for – very well, he was up to it. "I've had second thoughts, you see."

"I must say I thought it was all settled, all cut and dried, Gerald. I've made arrangements to move people in. I told you that."

"Well, you'll just have to unmake them."

There was a pause. His host twitched his soiled handkerchief in surrender, and smiled. "Ah well. No point in rushing things," he said. "Say no more, Gerald. I quite understand. Take your time."

Gerry felt obliged to speak again. He released his chair and nodded an ill-timed farewell. "Thanks for the lunch," he said. "See you again sometime, perhaps."

He turned and left the pub.

Chapter Three

The Errant Baronet

It was nine o'clock in the morning. Gerry had just left his rooms, freshly shaved and in clean clothes. He was going to the Post Office. On hearing his front door tried he stopped at the head of the stairs. He had secured the door with a stout wedge of wood and a folded newspaper. At first it held firm, but after a few more violent shoves it swung free. From his first floor landing Gerry watched his visitor enter and stand a moment in the grey light of the doorway. There was a drizzle outside, the deposit of a retreating November mist.

Sir Alec Webb, who had no umbrella, now stepped inside Claremont Villas and heeled the door to behind him. The door banged shut, unimpeded by Gerry's Guardian or his wedge of wood, then opened again and remained ajar. Such a dramatic entry! Sir Alec stood in the hallway smoothing his wet hair down into its monkish fringe. He took out a fresh, pressed linen handkerchief, dried his prescription spectacles, and dabbed some moisture from his face.

Gerry waited in stony silence on the landing.

Sir Alec put his handkerchief away and looked up, and seemed surprised – but pleasantly surprised - to find Gerry standing there above him. He bid a cheery good morrow and started up the broken stairs.

Gerry said nothing until his visitor had reached the step below.

"This is the second occasion you've seen fit to barge into my house, Mr Webb." Gerry announced. "This is my house. It is where I live. You have no more right of entry here than you would at Buckingham Palace. Old chap."

Sir Alec was in his greatcoat again, fastened to the neck over a high starched collar. To Gerry he looked like a Victorian missionary, standing there so upright on the broken stairs, his hand on the loosened banister. There was something very earnest, protrusive, insistent, about the set of his mouth. His full lips were red raw from the cold outside, but not at all sensual.

At Gerry's icy tone Sir Alec's face had become grave. His eyes stiffened behind his glasses.

"This is a squat, Gerry."

"This is a licensed squat, and I am the licensee."

"Oh, for goodness' sake."

"I am persona grata here, my friend. And you are persona non grata. The authorities know nothing of your intentions to move in here."

Gerry presumed that his visitor would take his 'authorities' seriously.

"Gerald, we've been through all this." Sir Alec's face was strained under his damp fringe, but only by the awkwardness of the situation. There was no trace about him of any fear or discomfiture. His voice was a steady drawl. "I reserved these premises long before you ever clapped eyes on them, Gerry. I have been tolerant of your indecisiveness so far, but I will not be tolerant of any deliberate obstruction. The Cooperative is moving into Claremont Villas. That, I'm afraid, is a statement of fact. This very morning I have an interview arranged here."

Gerry scowled. An interview? What on earth . . .?

Locked eyeball to eyeball he noticed that the prescription spectacles only had the appearance of the same: they were actually shinier and stronger framed, much more expensive.

"Whatever are you talking about?"

"Someone needs a job, Gerry. Someone wants to work. With unemployment figures as they are, you're not going to stand in his way, I trust?"

Behind his fancy glasses Sir Alec's bald eyes had narrowed. It was impossible to doubt his sincerity.

At which point a second person stepped through the front door and into the hallway below. He was a neat, alert looking man in his early twenties, with a thin face and furry haircut. He sniffed the damp air, twitched, and glanced around, as if he'd smelled a rat and wanted to ferret it out. In one hand he carried a ragged carpenter's tool bag, which he held at a slight distance from his person, away from his clean clothes. Despite the cold and damp he wore only a jean suit with a plain white t-shirt beneath his jacket. He looked first at the figure on the stairs, at the tall, sombre Sir Alec Webb, and then at the short, grim, older gentleman standing close by on the landing.

In turn these two stared down at him.

"Morning!" the young man called up breezily, ignoring

their severity. "I'm looking for a Mr Webb. Is either one of you . . . ?"

"I am Mr Webb." Sir Alec nodded down to the young man. "I am he. I am Alec Webb. And you are John Fitzroy, yes?"

"Correct, sir." Fitzroy looked all about Claremont Villas now, at the wrecked stairs, the burst walls and falling ceiling. His gaze slipped down the suspended banister and fell through the doorless door frames on the ground floor. "Is this the place needs the work?" He kicked aside Gerry's Guardian and lump of wood, ready to get started.

"Not immediately," said Sir Alec, with fruity authority. He glanced back at Gerry. "Do come up, John. We're on the second floor."

John Fitzroy picked his way nimbly up the staircase with his bag of tools. Gerry noted his cheap, fashionable baseball boots, done up with tigerish laces in stiff and waxy loops. He recognized, with some misgiving, the outmoded flair of the working class, the brief assertion that had guttered out a year or so ago. This was a suede-head, no less, successor to the brutalized, utilitarian skinhead. The young man's spring up the stairs spoke of energy, vigour, and a brittle optimism that might implode into aggression at any moment. When he passed Gerry on the landing he gave him a cheeky nod. But in fact there was no insolence, let alone menace in his eyes, and the vitality of the young man wounded Gerry, made him feel very old and weak and sad.

Curious, because this morning he had left his rooms full of a new hope; not an excited, agitated feeling, but a serene confidence about the future. The letter he'd written to Anna before the weekend had confirmed something within him. But now he saw how fragile his mood had been, how easily his sensibilities were shaken. Just the speed in this young man's step on the broken stairs, in his new baseball boots, brought the whole world crashing down about his ears again. Doubt. Depression. Alienation. His three sisters. Three sirens.

But why be so upset? Why? Whatever for? How ridiculous to be so susceptible, so suggestible.

It was true, though. When he had left his rooms, freshly shaved and in clean clothes, his empty shopping bag rolled in his hand, he had been ready for the world, he had had his own purpose, which had seemed meaningful and positive. He'd been going to the Post Office to see if any mail had been held back there, in case this were no longer a registered address, in case the Council had not rescinded its notice that no mail should be sent here not unless – but what utter nonsense! Of course every letter sent from all over the world if addressed here would arrive here, just as the bills did for the gas and electricity. What futility and stupidity and what abject hope was in this visit, to dally an hour or two in various queues at the Post Office in order to establish beyond doubt that which was perfectly obvious. Lunacy beckoning again. Anna's reply would arrive by the afternoon post, or certainly tomorrow. And if it didn't then he would telephone. He did not want to telephone – it was the last thing he wanted to do - but he would. After first post tomorrow morning he would seek Anna's answer on the telephone line. It was most unlike her, though, not to reply to a letter by return, particularly a letter of such import. She was punctilious about such things.

Gerry now found himself in a quandary. By his own hand he had taken away his principal reason for going out this morning. There was no urgent shopping to be done. Yet he would not, could not go back in, not with Mr Webb and his young guest now occupying the second floor. An interview? Why? What was that about, for goodness´sake?

He felt paralysis taking hold. Old demons worming their way in under innocent speculations. He took the broken stairs quickly, two at a time, helter-skelter, to escape himself. He must get out. He would go early today to the library. He'd read the papers. He must distract himself from himself.

Sir Alec Webb already knew which of the second floor rooms of Claremont Villas was to serve which purpose, but the room he wanted for interviews was in no fit state for occupancy. He was obliged to use the lighter and more spacious room at the end of the corridor, which he had assigned to be his Office. However, at the moment this room too was virtually unfurnished. There was just a couple of kitchen chairs that he had gathered from odd corners of the house.

"I do apologize for the décor," Sir Alec said, leading the young carpenter into the room. "We've only just acquired this property. Not had a chance yet to do much to it."

The carpenter looked about the room. The rotten sash windows, bloated skirting, uneven floor boards, handleless door.

"Developer, are you, Mr Webb?"

Sir Alec nodded and smiled broadly. "If you like. Of human resources."

The carpenter frowned at this cryptic answer, but pressed ahead chirpily.

"What's it all about then, this Cooperative? Caring and sharing is it? You scratch my back, I scratch yours?"

Sir Alec offered the young man a kitchen chair and sat down himself.

"Would you like to put down your tools?"

There was a brief silence, and then, as if lowering his guard, the carpenter set his tool bag on the floor and sat down. They faced each other, interviewee and interviewer, across the bag of tools. Sir Alec made no attempt to answer any of the carpenter's questions. Instead he smiled benignly and knitted his hands behind his head.

"I mean, can you put me in the picture? What's it all about?"

"Two Strong Arms?"

"Yeah," the carpenter nodded. He shifted in his kitchen chair. "What's it all about?"

"It's about Two Strong Arms, John."

Sir Alec's repetitions and silences unnerved the carpenter. He was full of doubts and tensions. He crossed his legs now, having had them set firmly on the bare boards of Sir Alec's 'Office'.

With the invitation to say a few words about Two Strong Arms, Sir Alec now assumed command of the interview. He unclasped his hands and lowered them to rest humbly in his aristocratic lap.

"I'd be delighted to respond most fully to your questions, or as fully as you require me to, John. I am myself the originator, the progenitor, if you will, of Two Strong Arms. Mine were the first biceps to be leant to the cause! . . ." Sir Alec allowed himself a mild chuckle at this self-serving play on words. He'd used this line many times, usually with some success. But not a flicker of amusement crossed John Fitzroy's face. If anything, following this remark, the carpenter's features became grimmer and sterner. "I started the organization a few years ago," Sir Alec resumed, "in response to what I saw as a bit of a national emergency . . ."

Sir Alec left space for some response. A question about the national emergency, perhaps. But not a sound came from his interviewee, nor did he make a movement of any kind.

"It seemed to me perfectly obvious, John, that there were scores of young people such as yourself - highly skilled, highly talented - who were not getting an even break in the job market, despite the best efforts of our friends in the Labour Party." Sir Alec leant forward. "Now, no matter what the unemployment statistics might indicate, there's stacks of work to be done, don't you think? Stacks of work. I mean real work. Such as fixing up this house. Redecorating it. Restoring it . . ." Sir Alec cast an expert eye around the empty, dirty room. "Restoring it to what it was originally meant to be, a residence of some standing for a large family, I should say. Really quite a respectable piece of Edwardian architecture. Part of the national heritage, if you like. So there's bags of work to be done. Anyone can see that. There are big jobs - like this place - and there are small jobs too, of course, that are more charitable, perhaps . . . Poor old Mrs Jones of Hampstead Garden calls up one afternoon. Can't get out so much these days. She wants a cat-flap thingy fitted in her front door - "

On this second example of the work to be done to address the national emergency, there came a movement, at last, an interruption from the carpenter -

"Er - not my line, Mr Webb. I don't want any of that, if that's what we're talking about. Cat-flaps. Mickey Mouse. If that's all you've got we're wasting our time."

The young carpenter's tone was final. He seemed to want to draw the meeting to a close already. Be done with it. He had lost faith in why he had come here this morning.

"I was merely demonstrating the variety of work which

needs to be done," Sir Alec said stiffly. "Big jobs or small jobs, they're all jobs that need doing."

"Right," the carpenter said, suddenly knowing how to proceed. "Let's have a look at your order book then, Mr Webb, and we'll see what we can do, shall we?"

Sir Alec sat back. Clearly, in the interests of sustaining a civil dialogue with this impatient young man, this rude young man, he was going to have to sacrifice much of his introduction. He considered himself pragmatic. So be it.

"The system is this, John. We advertise to undertake any job which can be done by the personnel currently in our employ." Sir Alec was now determined to impress the young carpenter with the size and scope of Two Strong Arms, with the breadth and strength of his Cooperative's embrace. The allusion to Mickey Mouse had been galling. "At the moment, for example, we have bricklayers, electricians, decorators, we have removals outfits, fly-posters, garbage shifters, mini-cabbers, pest-controllers, dog-catchers - "

"Hold it!"

This second interruption from the carpenter was more forceful, and was accompanied by a gesture, a raised flat palm, almost a fascist salute.

"Dog-catchers?"

Fitzroy's eyes narrowed. A nasty side of his nature was coming through: aggressive, vicious, snapping, uncontrollable. His lips thinned, baring disorderly and neglected teeth.

"Each to his own, John," Sir Alec resumed, treading gently, warily. "There's good work to be done catching strays, you know."

Fitzroy was blunt and angry now: "Get out of it!"

"I beg - "

"Get the fuck out of it!"

Fitzroy brushed away the dog-catchers and all the rest of Sir Alec's personnel as if they were so much sawdust on his jeans.

"I want the bottom line, Mr Webb. What you can offer, or I'm out of here. I've heard enough of this. For one morning."

It might have been expected that Sir Alec would be confounded by such an attack, but not at all. He had heard this kind of thing so many times, and much worse than this, much more personal. He'd seen the signs. It was no surprise.

"I can offer you work, Mr Fitzroy, and plenty of it."

He now had the young man's attention again.

"We have no carpenters at the moment and there's a backlog. We're also short of plumbers and glaziers, if you have any friends that way inclined. Before you interrupted I was going to tell you about our system. We man the telephone at the hours in the advertisements. Orders are logged in the register. We have a register. We have a roster."

The carpenter was lighting a cigarette. Exhaling the smoke, he threw in lightly, without thinking:

"Bully for you, m'lud."

As so many had done before him, John Fitzroy had slipped into rudely mimicking Sir Alec's accent. But Sir Alec's was a genuine accent, ingrained from infancy. There was little he could have done to change it even he'd wanted to. Which he did not. That would have been going too far. And Sir Alec was indeed an Old Gordonstounian, and had spent his formative years in the company of royalty, and he carried the airs and graces still that were his birthright. In fact, there was many a jape he could mention, touching on royal persons, that he liked to recount during these interviews: it was sometimes a weakness, sometimes a corrective duty, sometimes an acid test. But right now he pressed on - no anecdotes today, not with this fellow.

"Every worker - including myself - " Sir Alec resumed, "mans the switchboard once a fortnight for four hours. The system's simple, John. It's effective. It works. From there it's really down to you. Workers can call at the office at any hour of day to pick up jobs. The early worker gets the worm. Earlier workers get more worms." Webb leant forward earnestly again, pressing home some impalpable advantage. "Competition is fierce, John, as it should be. Once the job has been signed out from the order book, it is up to the individual worker to get on with it as soon as he or she possibly can. We want a quick turnover. I lay great stress on that."

Fitzroy looked sceptical about these laissez-faire conditions of employment.

"You mean I make up my own rates?"

"You make up your own rates, John." Webb sat back again. "It's your work. Your livelihood. Overcharge and people won't give you any work. Market forces, you see, John. Market forces."

Having given this answer Sir Alec smiled with a curious smugness, as if he'd been obliged to remind the carpenter of a fact of life the young man might find distasteful.

"The eternal verities apply," Sir Alec continued, with an open handed gesture, as if they were surrounded by them, the eternal verities, in this empty, dusty room. "And there's a seven per cent surcharge on your net profits which goes into Two Strong Arms." He wagged a finger. "You must remember that when totting up your accounts. It pays for the advertisements and the telephone."

The carpenter finished his cigarette and rubbed it out on the bare boards.

"Fair enough. So . . . What if I bodge it? What then?

What're the comebacks? Who's in charge? Where's the foreman? Who's the gov'nor?"

"Don't you even think about bodging it, John," said Sir Alec. "I'm the foreman. I'm the gov'nor."

Fitzroy snorted at this. He laughed openly in Sir Alec's face.

"You're fucking joking!"

"I'm the foreman." Again Sir Alec held steady. "I get rid of people if I have to, if they're bringing the organization into disrepute. I have that power and I have that right, as leader of Two Strong Arms."

The carpenter weighed up this idea, the pros and cons of it, finding his own angle.

"I see," he said, more to himself than Sir Alec.

Sir Alec smiled his complacent smile once more. "So, John, are you interested?"

"What's on the books?"

"Firstly, a few educational details, please, John."

The carpenter sighed and lifted his foot onto his knee. He inspected the sole of his new baseball boot. Discovering his cigarette butt lodged between the treads, he leant down and flicked it into a corner of the room. The soft tap of the butt hitting the skirting drew attention to the silence, to the dusty emptiness of the room, to the silence all around in the empty house, and in the damp November street outside. He looked up again at Webb and sighed, still very much inclined to take his leave.

"St. Jude's, Walthamstow. After that, did an apprenticeship for a year. Couldn't hack it. Decided to give it a go on my own. Life story."

"And how's it gone so far, John?"

"Not too bad at all. But there are always lean spells. That's what I don't like. That's why I pricked up my ears when my mum showed me this. Looked steadier."

"It can be. It can be." Sir Alec sat back expansively. "You know, I've often heard people like you talk about their education in that way, John. As if it meant nothing to them. It was a waste of time. Mine was rather different."

Fitzroy scowled. Where was this leading?

Sir Alec adjusted his spectacles, leant in towards his interviewee.

"You see, John, what I wonder is, did all that soft soap and kindness really do you much good?"

"Of course it did. What's that got to do with the order book?"

Sir Alec looked irritated. His voice took an impatient edge: "You see, John, I wonder if it really did do you any good. You didn't learn a great deal about manners, did you? My own school days were rather different, I'd have you know. Tougher, I should say. No half measures. No giving anything up. No room for anyone work-shy. If you didn't get on with things you were beaten by your fellows. And they beat you hard - believe me. I myself was beaten many times, John."

Frowning, the carpenter raised a hand again, half arrest, half surrender –

"Er - what're you telling me this for, Mr Webb?"

"There's a comparison to be made. Please do not interrupt me any more, John. Anyone work-shy was beaten. With a cane, a slipper, whatever came to hand - "

But John Fitzroy was on his feet.

"Now I get it. Now I got you." He pointed down at Sir Alec. "Not me, mate. Matey. I got you now. I'm out of here. I've had a bellyful of this." He picked up his tool bag and in a trice he was out the door. He shouted back at Webb from the landing.

"What a fucking waste of time that was!"

At the front door he met Gerry coming back from the

28

library, which did not open until eleven-thirty on Mondays, a fact that had slipped Gerry's shifting and shiftless mind. The young carpenter threw his bag onto his other arm and thumbed up the stairs. His face was red and angry.

"Who is that wanker?"

He shook his head as if trying to break free of the humiliation he'd just endured. He looked out to the grey street and muttered a stream of abuse under his breath. Gerry only caught a few words of it. The carpenter turned and seemed about to say something more to him, but did not. Some speculation had stalled him. He looked Gerry over with jumpy, puzzled eyes, struggling to make a connection. Then, without another word, he brushed by and set off down the pavement.

Gerry hesitated at the front door, watching Mr Fitzroy walk down Lonsdale Road. A neat, brisk, blue figure in the grey street, with his bag of tools held away from him, threading between some shabby vehicles standing in the gutter, and crossing the road to the corner shop.

No van, Gerry thought. Or van broken down, maybe.

The carpenter turned the corner and was gone. Forever, presumably.

Gerry's curiosity about what Mr Webb could have done to so get under this young man's skin was displaced by a need to do some mischief himself. He had a Guardian in his hand. He furled it and tucked it under his arm. This he could not resist. He eased the front door to, tiptoed up the stairs, and made his way stealthily to the second floor.

But on the landing the bare boards creaked and gave him away. When he arrived Sir Alec was already drawing himself up from an attitude of defeat at the filthy window.

"Ah, there you are, Gerry . . ."

Gerry stopped just inside the doorway. "How did it go? Your interview."

"Very well," Sir Alec answered gamely. "Very well indeed." He glanced about his Office with an air of detachment. "We shall have to do something about this place. I'll get some help."

"From the Cooperative?"

Sir Alec turned again to face Gerry.

"Yup . . ."

"Perhaps Mr Fitzroy can help too, eh?" Gerry said. "Good grief! So you've given him a job? Just like that? Terrific! Who'd have thought it? Out of work one minute, gainfully employed the next. Pension. Paid holidays. National insurance - "

"No, Gerry." Sir Alec jutted out his jaw. "It didn't work out. Can't use him, I'm afraid."

"Oh no. Why on earth not?"

"Inflexible. Won't adapt."

"Really? But he struck me as a most amenable young man. Salt of the earth."

"That's why it went well, Gerald," Webb replied, his voice now a confident drawl again. "We got beneath all that."

"I see."

Sir Alec looked again out of the window and squinted at its dusty light. Some weak November sunshine was breaking through. "I'd have liked to take him on, but I couldn't. One has to be realistic."

"Indeed," Gerry echoed, "one has to be realistic." He tapped his Guardian on his thigh. "Have you any more interviews today, or is that the lot?"

"No more today, Gerald. I'll leave you in peace."

Sir Alec approached the doorway where Gerry stood tapping and furling his Guardian. When he was just a step away Gerry spoke again.

"I met our Mr Fitzroy on the way out. Do you know

what he called you? He called you a wanker. A wanker. What do you make of that?"

"One gets hardened to it, Gerald." Sir Alec smiled and passed by. He called back again over his shoulder as he negotiated the broken stairs: "One soon gets hardened to all that!"

Chapter Four

The Prodigal

Gerry was reluctant to burn his bridges and quit his lodging altogether. It was tempting to do so. It would have been very pleasing to inform Alec Webb, on his next visit, that he could move into Claremont Villas, by all means, with or without his Cooperative, with or without Gerry's cooperation, whenever he pleased, and good luck to him. And to add, moreover, that having been through his little late-life crisis, having done his penance, endured his trial by ordeal, he was going on holiday to Provence, where he also proposed to spend a long and happy retirement. Yes, to imagine speaking to Webb of these matters and in that tone was indeed alluring. But the memory of three months past, when he had actually spent a few nights without a roof over his head, was as fresh and vivid and distinctly unpleasant as yesterday's encounter with Webb himself. That salutary exposure to the elements, and they had been the elements of August, not November, had made Gerry a more wary man.

And he had changed in other ways. His attitude towards money had changed fundamentally. This came from necessity of course, living on state handouts, but he also saw the relativities around him in a different light these days. As he walked the streets of Notting Hill and Kensington and West Kensington, it now seemed to him that the English bourgeoisie - in whose class, until recently, he would have counted himself, of course – these ordinary middle-class souls that he encountered on the pavement, or at the Belisha beacon, strolling about in their warm clothes, or driving about in their warm cars - it seemed to him that these people took their good fortune rather too readily for granted. There was something quite impenetrable about the English middle-classes, Gerry had decided. It was in their eyes, a certain steadiness and solidity of gaze, an impenetrable assurance, a smugness. They seemed to regard their world, and everything in it, as an entirely personal accomplishment. Out of some habit of mind the rôle of provenance, providence, luck, best of British, was not admitted. Gerry considered that in contrast he had learned some humility. The gamble he had taken in casting himself out had been reckless, no doubt, foolhardy even; but it had been the right thing to do *for him*. No one else he knew would ever have had the guts to do such a thing. When, at his wit's end, quite in despair, he'd mumbled something about 'chucking in his hand' to his GP, or 'doing away with himself somehow or other', the good doctor had just laughed. Laughed in his face. A soft and fruity, rich and mellow, serve at room temperature kind of laugh –

"Oh I say, now really, my dear chap, one doesn't want to do anything rash now, hmmn? . . ."

This, even when he had reached a point where something had to change, to give, a risk of some sort had to be taken. And he had brought that change about himself, he'd taken his own wild gamble. Why should he not feel proud of that, of what he had done? Without pills, without expense, without burdening the taxpayer or taking up anyone's precious time, he had seen off his dark night of the soul with just a little honest-to-goodness, commonsensical, hair-shirted self-denial.

Anna would indeed find him a changed man. To her what he had done would still look like heartless folly, but he would return vindicated. Purged. The gamble had paid off. That much was self-evident.

He had tried telephoning her but without success. Directory Enquiries said the number was out of use. More than that they were not at liberty to say. Of course this provoked speculation: no reply to his letter; telephone number changed - What had happened? Was everything all right? But his confidence that Anna *was* all right, safe and secure in the house he had left, surrounded by the goods and chattels they had accumulated over thirty years' middle-class husbandry, thirty years of childless married life, that basic confidence was unshaken. Solid as the house itself. Given a moment's thought it was quite understandable that she should have changed the telephone number, gone ex-directory, perhaps. There must have been some fuss after his departure, once the news was abroad: calls from neighbours, calls from colleagues at school. The Head, no doubt, and maybe his old Head of Department, would have telephoned to pass on their token concern, before relapsing into indifferent silence. There would have been a visit from some cub reporter from *The Eastern*

Daily Press, no doubt. It would all have been far too much for Anna, who had always found dealings with his colleagues distasteful, and with the world at large fatiguing, enervating. Getting rid of the old telephone number must have been an immediate necessity. It had been stupid of him to imagine he could just pick up the receiver in a public telephone booth, put in his two pence piece, and dial back to the old life. There had to be some changes, for goodness' sake.

But that said it was equally certain there could have been no major change. Anna enjoyed good health and he had left her fit and well. She was given to her irritable moods, but she was not one for sitting around feeling sorry for herself or getting depressed. She'd always been most intolerant of the least sign of that sort of thing. *There's many a soul in this country a lot worse off than you are. You've a decent home, a good job and you'll get a fair pension at the end of the day. You should be grateful for all of that.* Thank you, Anna. Yes, Anna. By some means or another she would have passed the time - just as she had all his working days, all his working years, his working life. Waiting for things, passing her time, was something she was good at. She most certainly would not have gone anywhere. She had always been an unwilling traveller, particularly on her own. And there couldn't have been any terrible accident, God forbid, because if there had some effort would have been made to find him, which would not have been at all difficult. A morning's elementary detective work would have traced him to Claremont Villas. He had made no attempt to hide himself or cover his tracks. In fact, during his first few days of homelessness, he had experienced a quiet disappointment that no such effort to find him had been made. He had actually drifted into a police station once, but had drifted out again in a mood of bitter self-contempt, without turning himself in or making any enquiry about himself.

Observing what he knew well to be an unnecessary, even neurotic precaution, he locked up his bedroom in Claremont Villas as usual and protected that little refuge. It was sweet to imagine that tomorrow morning he might find this key on the dressing table in his real bedroom, this petty symbol of a different world. He would stop and frown at it, no doubt. He would toss it in the air and catch it again, then throw it away, be done with it. But no. In the event he would hang on to it, not as sentimental memento, nor as salutary reminder, but as something which bore witness to all he had been through. The keeping together of body and soul these last few months had been no mean feat. Dealing with the vagaries of the state benefit system, into which he must have poured God only knew how many tens of thousands of pounds over the years, for a quite derisory return in his hour of need, had been a challenge of labyrinthine complexity. Survival of the fittest. But at least he knew now what it was like at the bottom of the heap. Scroungers? Not really. They had a terrible time of it. A bloody awful time of it. He would no longer, with that wry humour which had won him so much admiration in the staff room, make those tiresome jokes that began, *Come the revolution* . . .

No. He could well see the point of a revolution now of some description, so long as it didn't spread to Ipswich before he got home.

So he felt very differently leaving Claremont Villas this morning, not setting off for the library or on some circuitous walk, but on his way *home*. Home! He had not allowed himself to savour some of the delights ahead until now. Sleeping in his own bed. Drinking freshly ground coffee. Eating decent meals. Cooking! . . . He was a good cook and knew an impressive range of Provençal dishes. He'd always cooked the weekend meals, while Anna had provided during the week – microwave stuff, more often than not, in more recent years. She'd never liked the kitchen. Too small, she said. She kept out of it all weekend. Out of his way, she said. But could he still remember all his dishes? All the herbs and spices? A pinch of this and a pinch of that? Or would he be forced back to fumbling through the recipe books? Of course he could remember them! All of them. He would go with Anna to Sainsbury's and buy the plumpest free range bird in the store and cook a chicken Provençal they'd never, ever forget.

He crossed Lonsdale Road and stopped to look back at Claremont Villas for the last time. He looked at the front door, slightly ajar and badly scarred around the lock where it had been jemmied by Webb or one of his strong armed henchmen; he looked up at the windows of his floor, which were reasonably clean, except for his bedroom window that he couldn't get at from the outside. His makeshift curtains, thin and shabby, hung from nails he'd hammered into the moulding. Above, on the second floor, now Webb's floor, the windows were filthy and bore the cross of the condemned building. That was rather sad, because even up until the fifties, perhaps, until it had been chopped up into bedsits, Claremont Villas must have been the source of much pride as a family home.

He dropped his head and sighed. Well, thank God it was all over, anyway. This episode. He was indeed, at last, *ready* to go home.

He could have enjoyed an Inter-City from Liverpool Street, with perhaps a royal cooked breakfast in the buffet car to boot, such a treat was just about affordable given this was a one way ticket, but the coaches were less than half the price of the trains and this kind of economizing was now ingrained in his nature. So he went to Victoria. He would not be extravagant, even on a celebratory journey of this kind. What a change Anna would see in him! He'd been wont to spend money wildly at times. It had been a way of distracting himself, of releasing the anxiety work generated in him. When the torments of school became intolerable he would insist they went away to some hotel in the Lake District for a weekend, or that they buy some wretched gadget that he would fiddle with right through until Sunday evening, when the storm clouds gathered. Ah, all those Sunday evenings. Good heavens, how had he endured – how many? - a thousand, or so? Thirteen hundred? But was that all? Thirteen hundred Sundays and one's career was over? Absurd, in a way, the whole thing. Ridiculous, the small sad waste of time.

At Victoria he made an effort to dispel both gloomy reflection and optimistic fantasy and apply himself to the practical matters in hand. He went to the public toilets to check his appearance. Did he look different? Did he look a new man?

The toilets were beneath the concourse. There was a turnstile. More expense. And he didn't even need the toilet, just a mirror.

With so many secondhand clothes stalls and charity shops in London these days it wasn't difficult to fit yourself up if you took the time and trouble. His schoolmaster's Harris Tweed, complete with leathered cuffs and elbows, now dry-cleaned, was as respectable as it had been when it formed part of his uniform. He had on a pair of decent light brown trousers, of a rather inferior material, it must be said, and rather too light, almost beige, if the truth were told, but perfectly acceptable. They complemented the all-leather brogues he'd picked up in a

Sue Ryder gift shop for a couple of pounds. He was clean shaven and he'd invested in a cheap haircut from a traditional barber's. He had worn his hair long for a while. The bulk of it had taken away the shape of his head. With this unfussy haircut his face had its neat, triangular outline once more, and his forehead was clear of the stray locks he'd put up with for far too long. He lifted his chin and looked himself up and down in the full length mirror. He buttoned up the Harris Tweed at the middle and tugged down the hem of the jacket.

There had been some weight loss. So much the better. He was an altogether leaner, fitter individual. *Leaner, fitter* - he liked those comparatives. They were Mrs Thatcher's new words. *Leaner, fitter.* She was making ground with them too, against the flabby Callaghan gang. There stood before him a respectable and presentable man in his late fifties. A man whose features were sensitive, delicate even - but not weak. He was confident, self-possessed.

One or two other people were trying to use the mirror now. A young black with fearsome dreadlocks was edging his way here and there into the spaces of the glass Gerry left spare, but Gerry did not move for him, nor for anyone else. He remained exactly where he was, full square in front of the mirror. He conceded nothing. He stared into his own brown eyes. Stared long and hard. Here was the chief change.

"Move over, pops."

The young black was getting impatient.

"Come on. Get lost."

But Gerry did not move over. He would not get lost. His eyes were no longer the soft, brown, vulnerable eyes which, off guard, were shot through with anxiety and self-doubt. These eyes were firm, clear, direct. That haunted look had gone. These were the eyes he should have had throughout his career, eyes that stopped misbehaviour with a look, no accompanying words required. He tried out a haughty, overbearing glance on the young black fellow in the mirror, and said out loud:

"There have been some changes all right!"

The young man seemed unsurpised.

"Sure there have. Now get lost."

Gerry brushed past him, slipped the turnstile and seized the stairs two at a time.

Leaner, fitter.

At Ipswich he stepped down from the coach with a lightness that suggested the confidence he'd felt at the beginning of the journey had not deserted him, but Ipswich town centre had always been a place where, for as far back as he could remember, Gerry had felt ill at ease, anxious, afraid even. Over the years there had been several occasions when he had been out shopping and there had been 'incidents' with boys from his school. Boys had barracked him from across the street, or hailed him from across a store. "Hey! Delaporter! Where's yer daughter?" Oh, his ghastly name! His horrible, pretentious, bourgeois name! What a curse it had always, always been, and what a gift to those brutes. If Mrs Delaporte were with him, rather than temper their abuse she would excite it. They were quick to drag her in: "Out with the old Mrs, eh? Gonna buy her a peep-hole, eh?" It was no use ignoring it, trying to pick through another row of Harris Tweeds or Clydellas or Vyellas, pretending that the abuse was directed at someone else. He would be the only one trying to ignore it. And of course, after the first few taunts, his tormentors moved on to their chants, their declensions from the rude and lewd to the obscene:

"Delashit!"
"Delatit!"
"Delaprick!"
"Delabollocks!
"Delafuck!"
"Delacunt!"

Leading his wife by the arm Gerry would seek a quick exit from the situation. A scene such as this had been enough to stop him returning to the town centre for several weeks. There would be another weekend in the Lake District and after that Gerry would be housebound. In his boredom he would find odd jobs around the house; fiddling, unnecessary improvements which he loathed doing and which resulted in things not being improved but impaired, because he was not a DIY man.

As he was retired now, any encounter with such yobs could be dealt with on his own terms, and was no longer anything to be feared. He would give them as good they gave him. He'd match them obscenity for obscenity, as loud as they liked. He'd enjoy that. He'd soon fix *them*! And yet, to be back in this place, Ipswich bus station, was still undeniably just a little unnerving. Gerry was thirsty. He would have liked to stop for five minutes in the bus station cafeteria, but he did not do so, could not do so. He pressed on and sought out the bus stage for his district, only to discover that he had just missed a bus - yet still he did not turn back to the cafeteria. And he was thirsty, very thirsty. But that bus station cafeteria had always been a favourite hangout for a particular kind of youth. Cursing the bus service as unreliable anyway, he decided to walk. He was used to long walks and the secondhand brogues were a good fit. He had to keep on the move. If he stopped for a moment some vital momentum might be lost.

He had tried several times to formulate what he would

say to Anna. It was reminiscent of trying to prepare a lesson at school, something he'd always postponed until the time was upon him, and then accomplished, despite its pointlessness, in a state of abject panic. What on earth would he say to her? After the initial emotion, the outpourings, the turmoil, the huggings and clingings, for which he must be prepared - after all that, when it was time to break the impasse, the emotional deadlock, what would he actually say to her?

As he drew closer to home, to his cluster of terraced streets, any misgivings he had were expunged by an intoxicating and boyish excitement. He realized that the future was much more valuable to him now than it had been when he retired in the summer. And how distant did his life in London suddenly seem, its petty nuisances and anxieties, with these solid and familiar streets before him. Alec Webb, indeed. Good grief! Was there really such a fellow? Two Strong Arms! Was all that really still going on in the nation's capital, the seat of government, just a couple of hours away by Express coach? Webb's was a face of England to be swiftly forgotten, and yet how much more thankful he was for the prospects before him because he knew that face of England now, and the face of England's poor, and he'd seen through all that awful class-bound nonsense that held everything in place. Such was the buoyancy and excitement he felt about these insights the idea came to him that Anna was to be thanked - yes, thanked! - for allowing him his petty dénouement to the tragi-comedy of his career.

And here he was, at last, at the head of good old Rosebery Road, that which hath the antique spelling. Here he had to stop and be still. Halt. Check the excitement. A distinction had forked his thoughts. This road he stared down, where he had spent more or less all his working life (he had refused to climb the property ladder so that he and Anna could afford their summers in Provence), this road where he had existed for thirty years, that poky terraced house where he had gone through the functions of life, where he had eaten his sacks of muesli, drunk his barrels of coffee, tea and wine, where he had bathed and showered his ageing body year by year, where he had excreted his tons of faeces and tankers of urine, where he had had sex (though never enough, and not at all in recent years: somehow Anna had persuaded him this was the lot of all men), this house where he had returned each evening with his briefcase full of scruffy exercise books, and from whence he had left the next morning without opening a single one of them, this house, this road, this England - good grief, this was no place of fondness, just disaffection pure and simple, just the site of one more endless, meaningless struggle for the pay cheque. No. All the excitement he had felt on approaching this place was to do with prospects beyond it, not the place itself. Surely that was a sobering thought, that no memory of joy or even contentment could be attached to this Rosebery Road. Good heavens, the misery of paying one's way! He looked down the road and it seemed to darken under the cast iron November skies, and that tunnelled darkness was the prevailing truth of the place. He had spent his life fleeing down tunnels of anxiety, briefcase in hand, towards a light that had never been better than dull, dull, dull.

There was a stiffness which came from anger in his walk as he started down the street towards his home. Suddenly he did not feel like talking. He did not even feel like meeting his wife. He did not want all the emotional excess. He wished he could simply open his door, go into his living room, and sit down on the sofa, and just be quiet for a very long time.

In this mood of absorption he stepped up the path to the front door, found the key on the ring, inserted it, turned it, and pushed the door wide. He stepped over the threshold and closed the door gently behind him. He could hear movement in the house. It was from the kitchen. The sound of the cutlery drawer being pushed shut. The clatter of the green plastic tray shunting in the drawer. Then nothing. Silence.

Anna.

A tap started.

Stopped.

Washing her coffee mug after elevenses. Pensively shaking out the drips.

"Gerald, is that you?" He could almost hear it. Prepare yourself, Gerry, he told himself. Prepare yourself, old boy. The turmoil. The huggings, the clingings. They had never been the most demonstrative of couples, but perhaps on this occasion . . .

A small, dark woman, shoulder length hair, about forty, not unattractive, appeared at the end of the hallway. She had a dish towel over one arm. On seeing Gerry standing on the doormat, the front door closed behind him, she looked shocked. She muttered something in another tongue - Spanish? Portuguese? - and retreated to the kitchen again. He heard her open the back door and call into the garden.

Gerry stood silently, his keys dangling in his hand. His mind was in wilful suspension. He refused to speculate about what this meant. The explanations, nothing too untoward, of course, would pour in from outside, not haemorrhage from inside.

A stocky, middle-aged, swarthy man, the husband presumably, came to the kitchen doorway and stopped dead. He stared at Gerry, looked him up and down. His gaze lighted on the keys dangling in Gerry's hand and he frowned. The woman, still standing in the kitchen doorway, just behind her husband, started saying something softly, discreetly. But her husband waved her into silence and came forward himself. He stopped near Gerry and gave him a neutral nod, then passed him by, turned and went upstairs. Halfway up he stopped again and looked down at Gerry:

"Un momentito, eh? Okay?"

Gerry nodded courteously. All would become clear. In a minute. A momentito. All would become clear.

There was some exchange in broken English upstairs and Gerry heard a young man's voice up there, from right above him. He looked up to the ceiling, to the yellowing whitewash and the plain moulding. The voice came from his bedroom. A young man's voice, from inside his bedroom. It was a brusque voice, cutting the other man off, and then there was a smack of some sort - a *smack!* - the sound of a hand smacked down on a table, perhaps.

Then: "All right, all right! I'll deal with it . . . I'll *bloodywell* deal with it! . . . For goodness' sake what's fucking next!"

The sound of steps on the landing above.

A tall, curly-haired, heavily built man in his late twenties or early thirties came down the stairs. He was doing up a pair of crumpled grey trousers. He wore a plain white shirt, open at the neck to several buttons down. A pair of ancient sandals exposed his knobbly ankles and large yellow heels. He was unshaven, his hair was tousled and his face was lined on one side as if he'd just got out of bed. He came down to within four steps of the foot of the stairs and stopped there, leaning on the banister. Gerry noted a tongue of white shirt trapped at the top of his fly.

After he'd stopped, after a noticeable time lag, two or three seconds perhaps, a very powerful and oniony stink of body odour rolled down the last four steps into the hallway. It was so extraordinary, this stink, the power of it, that Gerry had to stop himself yielding to it, taking a step backwards. Nothing less than a stench. Quite ghastly. And it was intensifying all the time. Oh my word - how it intensified! It belonged to this young man, yet he was so blithely unaware of it, and so unashamed - standing there, nonchalantly leaning on the banister - that it was like some kind of gesture from him, a friendly salutation. Something he offered perfect strangers, like Gerry Delaporte, without a thought, whenever they called, whenever they came home. So hospitable. My home is your home.

Well, thank you very much, sir!

The young man stood still on the stairs. A big fellow. A big slouch. But haughty. He stood there, and his haughty smell stiffened in the silence of the hallway until it had a presence of its own, a permanence, a shape, a form, a formality.

The other man, the dark man – so many strangers in his house! - had stopped halfway down the stairs, and remained there, upwind of his smelly emissary, stooping and crook-kneed and looking rather sorry for himself for some reason.

At last the young man spoke:

"What is it, pops? What's the problem?"

Move over, pops. Get lost.

But I am lost, Gerry thought. I am lost in my own home. He opened his mouth and emitted a pant, the start of a laugh that could never be laughed. But he said nothing.

"What's up, pops? Out with it. Come on. You can do it."

"I live here."

"No you don't, mate. We live here." The young man now noticed the keys in Gerry's hand. "Where did you get those from? Did you find them? Did someone give them to you?" His voice was gentle and a touch patronizing. Gerry felt as if he were perceived as someone infirm. All his grooming had been to no avail, then. The dry cleaning of the Harris Tweed. The polishing of the brogues. The beige trousers. The haircut. All to no avail. He was seen as infirm and he felt infirm. He wanted to put the young man right, set the record straight, but his mind had seized. Down to his side was a new telephone table, a mock-antique affair with curved legs of stained wood and a green leather seat, hemmed with shiny brass tacks. Pretentious rubbish. It was not his. There was no telephone on it. It was completely unfamiliar to him. Yet the rest of the house was entirely familiar. The wallpaper and the curtains were unquestionably his. This was his house. But the telephone table, that was not his. And there was something on it that drew back his eye. It was an elastic-banded bundle of letters. The uppermost letter of the bundle was addressed to his wife, and - ah, the pity of it! - it was in his own hand!

Now Gerry corrected himself, for the enlightenment of anyone who might understand in the assembled company.

"I used to live here."

The young man's mouth opened and he nodded. Now he could begin to deal with the situation.

"You used to live here."

"That's right," Gerry said. "I lived here for more than thirty years. I lived here for all of my working life. For my entire career I lived here. I went to work from this house in the morning, and returned from work to this house in the evening. For thirty years. From and to this house. To and from this house."

"Ahh . . ." The man nodded again and puckered his lips thoughtfully. "I get you, now . . ."

"I hung that wallpaper," Gerry added, encouraged,

raising his hand to point at the wallpaper above the stairs. The house keys dangled and jangled in the silence of the hallway. "That wallpaper. With the motif of violets and cornflowers." But no sooner had he said this than he knew this kind of assertion was both meaningless and uncalled for. He lowered his hand.

The Spanish couple, if that's what they were, were frowning from their different vantage points, but seemed to have grasped the essence of what had transpired in this slow, repetitive exchange. Gerry decided that the young man must be a tenant of this couple, must be subletting a room from them, and that the couple were émigrés, not from Spain or Portugal but from South America; they'd fled military regime in one of those ghastly Latin American countries, and had come through all manner of horrors and indignities, but had now found a haven of peace and asylum here, in his house, in *his* house, at 13 Rosebery Road, Ipswich. How extremely fortunate!

The tenant's eyes narrowed and he frowned too. Then he cocked his head: "Are you . . . Mr Delaporter?"

"Yes," Gerry closed his eyes and nodded. "Yes. I am Mr Delaporter."

"There's some mail for you." The tenant came down the last few stairs, stepped across the hallway and picked up the wad of letters from the telephone table. His sudden movement, close to Gerry, his bending down, disturbed fresh currents of his awful smell. He peeled back the first letter to read the name on the next (a typed, official looking letter) then let Gerry's letter flap back. "The first one's for your wife. Or your daughter?"

Delaporter, where's your daughter?

Gerry shook his head. "We had no children."

"For your wife, then."

Gerry said nothing. Lost in sliding introspection.

48

"Or your mother? Anna?"

"No. My mother is dead. That's my wife's name. I wrote that letter, as a matter of fact."

The tenant ignored this unnecessary complication, almost as if he knew Gerry were telling a lie. "But the rest are for you. Six or seven of them."

He offered the bundle to Gerry who took it from him. Gerry stared down at his own handwriting on the uppermost envelope. The pity of it.

"We couldn't forward them because there was no address, you see. Some of those were marked urgent. I phoned the agent but he said there was no forwarding address."

"The agent?"

"The estate agent."

"You rent the house?"

"No. They bought it," he said, with a nod to the couple behind him. "I rent from them."

There was a moment's deafening silence, absolute stillness.

"But they could not have bought it," Gerry glanced at the foreign couple, who stood side by side in his hallway now; the man had come down the stairs without his noticing. They looked different. The danger had passed and they were losing interest in Gerry, in his life, which had its history here. Gerry looked at the tenant as if he were being obtuse, a dunce in the class. His tone became stern. What the tenant had said was absurd, laughable: "They could not have bought this house, sir, because I never sold this house. It is my house. My house!"

The young man shrugged. That was beyond him.

"I don't know anything about that. You'll have to take that up with the agent. We don't know anything about that." He nodded at the letters. "Maybe they'll explain something for you. You go down and see the agent, see what he says. Ebbages. North Street. Look, sign's still outside. Sort it out with them."

Gerry turned. Through the frosted glass of the front door he could indeed make out some blurred bands of white and yellow. A signboard. For sale. Sold. How could he have missed that on his way in? How? Quite simple, really. By means of the same subliminal shuttering device that had stopped anything too ugly, momentous or true ever troubling his retina for the whole of his stupid, pointless, useless life! Oh, come on! Enough of this! Sold? Sold! *Sold!* It was preposterous!

But when Gerry looked back at the tenant he knew that the young man, for all his obtuseness, for all his stink, was absolutely right, it was time to go, there was nothing further to be gained from this visit.

"There's been a terrible mistake," Gerry said, "and your position here, I regret - " he looked past the tenant to the foreigners – "all your positions here - I mean to say, that is, *none* of your positions here - is at all safe. Is secure. I'm afraid. No matter what horrors and indignities you may have suffered, no matter what unhappiness and loneliness you may have endured."

"What?"

"There's been a terrible mistake, you see." He faced the young man again. "But you're right. You're quite right. I shan't trouble you any further. I shall go to Ebbages. I shall take my leave. For the moment. But I'll be back shortly. You can be certain of that. But for now I take my leave." He turned to go but as he did so he felt the tenant's heavy hand on his shoulder.

"Would you mind giving us the keys, pops?"

Gerry turned again and looked into the tenant's eyes. They were mild. He didn't mean to harm or offend. He was only doing what was reasonable under the circumstances. With him standing so close, hand raised to receive the keys, Gerry caught his smell full on. Something beyond body odour, too sharp for sweat. Something to do with rot. Foot rot, flesh rot. Fungi. And he was stinking up his house. *His* home. Quite unforgivable. But Gerry nodded and surrendered his keys.

"May I trouble you for a glass of water?"

The tenant, keys in hand, gave a one-sided, concessionary smile.

He led the way past the landlord and landlady, who looked about to protest.

"Quiet," the tenant commanded.

Inside the kitchen he took a glass from the draining rack, filled it, and gave it to Gerry. Gerry drank, and looked around as he drank. The draining rack was laden with his old crockery: the willow pattern, plate after plate of it, but some plates chipped now. There was his coffee mug, the expensive one from Clough Head. Elevenses. The kitchen itself was exactly as he'd left it. Oatmeal units. The big, ageing microwave. The single sink he'd always meant to replace with white enamel – the French look. On this side of the drainer was his wooden-handled fruit knife, out of its block.

Without a thought he snatched it up - but the tenant's hand was instantly on his wrist.

"*IT'S MY KNIFE!*" Gerry screamed. He smashed his glass on the floor and tried to push and punch the tenant off him but the tenant was far too strong for him, and squeezed and squeezed until he released the knife. It clattered in the empty sink. He pulled Gerry round by the wrist and whipped his arm behind his back -

"That's enough of you!"

He frogmarched Gerry past the landlord and landlady,

now standing at the kitchen door, and down the hallway.

"It's all right," Gerry muttered. "No need for this. No need."

At the door the tenant hesitated, apparently unable to manage the next manoeuvre single-handed. He relaxed, let Gerry's hand drop, then stepped back out of range.

"Out you go. Now."

Without turning Gerry opened the door and stepped outside, then shut the door behind him in that ordinary, habitual way, as if he were going out to buy a newspaper or a pint of milk. He walked slowly to the end of the path, past the unmissable white and yellow Ebbages signboard, with its loud red SOLD sticker slapped diagonally across the middle.

This was a wholly new feeling.

To have nothing.

This was very new.

To have *nothing.*

He stopped on the pavement the other side of the picket gate. His wrist was throbbing and his shoulder hurt, but he was unharmed. He shut his eyes and thought of Anna, his wife. But no, he could not do that, not yet. Opening his eyes again he sensed movement at the net curtains of the front window behind him, the only movement in the still and silent street, but he did not turn.

Chapter Five

Recourse to Law

"Ah. Now that is not my signature, you see."

They were both standing on the client's side of the desk. Mr Adam Maidment, the solicitor, a very slim man in his late thirties, was dressed entirely in black. Neat, tight black. Gerry took him for a bit of a dandy, but a provincial dandy. He stood with his arms braced on the desk staring down at a copy of the conveyancy contract for 13 Rosebery Road, Ipswich. Gerry felt a touch self-conscious about his beige trousers here in the solicitor's office, next to the thin solicitor all in black, but otherwise he remained plausible enough, he believed, in his secondhand clothes and polished brogues. He stood close by Mr Maidment, also with his head down, poring over the document, the legal proof. The vendors' signatures were there, his wife's and his own. The forgery was good, Gerry considered, but not so very good. The 'p' and the final 'e' were wrong: the 'p' too sloped and refined, altogether too dignified, and then the 'e' half undone by the underline that whipped back from it in a pretentious curlicue. Good heavens, it really was so ornate! To be quite honest, after thirty years of marriage, he would have thought she could have done better. Or was the exaggeration of his signature there deliberately to taunt him, mock him, with its whipped up, florid pretension? Could that be it? Could it? Was it as subtle, as spiteful, as that? Was that hatred then, in that flourish, in that thin black curvy line, with that most definite and redundant full stop? Yes. That's what it was. Hatred. Well, then. On the whole, when all was said and done, excellent work, Anna. 10/10. Go straight to the top of the form. And the simple, humble signatures of the purchasers were there, all in order: Juan and Pepita Peiriah. And the signatures of the witnesses were there, though very difficult to make out. Their addresses were unfamiliar. Bogus presumably. The Peiriahs would have done whatever she told them to do, of course.

"But it is witnessed, Mr Delaporte."

This response from the solicitor exasperated Gerry. "You know how people witness these things! They pop round to the neighbours and it's done during the adverts!" Gerry tapped the offending document firmly with his forefinger. "I was never there. I was not at home in August. Not at home. To anyone. I was not at home!"

"But it is witnessed." The solicitor looked up at him from over his golden half-moon glasses. Such decorative authority! In a different era they would have been pince-nez, or a phoney monocle. Gerry frowned, concerned that he was missing a subtlety here. "It wasn't witnessed. That's what I'm saying. No one witnessed me signing that document because I never signed it. That signature is a forgery, sir!"

The solicitor jutted forth his jaw. His eyes closed a second on his own impatience. "But it *is* witnessed."

"Will you please stop saying that!"

"Mr Delaporte," the solicitor said, removing his half-moons with practised ease, something he must have seen on television, on some costume drama - "*how* people arrange for the document to be witnessed and by whom it is witnessed is their own affair. We accepted this, as we do all conveyancy contracts submitted by the vendors, in good faith. Now, if you wish to support your allegation with proceedings against Mrs Delaporte, we shall be happy to look into the possibilities of such proceedings on your behalf. But only after Mrs Delaporte has been traced, of course, and that is a matter for the police. That's as much as I can say."

Gerry ran his tongue nervously around his dry lips. This man was quite unbelievably unhelpful. This man who'd sold his house. When Gerry spoke again he did so with calm and quiet emphasis.

"I have lost *everything* I own."

The solicitor stood upright, the conveyancy contract in his hands, and, head lowered, retreated once more behind his desk. He sat down.

Gerry continued, showing an uncharacteristic lack of restraint. "Everything I own, everything, my entire house and every stick of furniture therein, has been stolen from me, by my own *wife*!"

"So you say." The solicitor stroked his right ear. "Mr Delaporte, I suggest you go to the police."

"And tell them what?"

"I do not know, but I cannot help you further here." The solicitor cleared his throat and continued with some finality. "It is a matter for the police to trace your wife, and only when they have done so will it be worth your while taking your case any further. Out of consideration for your distress there will be no charge for this consultation, but I must advise you that I have many people to see this afternoon. We shall have to draw this interview to a close."

Gerry stood very upright where he was, supporting what dignity he could in his Harris Tweed and his secondhand brogues, and his inferior beige trousers, that he knew had completely lost their crease. But this was such a poor show.

"You really are being most unhelpful."

Mr Maidment shrugged. "Mr Delaporte, before one can do anything at all the police must establish exactly what has happened. That is police work, not the work of a solicitor. These are simply the facts of the matter, no matter how unpalatable. If I appear unsympathetic, I am sorry."

This man was a disgrace to his profession, no doubt, but Gerry knew he would get no further. He was defeated here. He made his way to the door, then turned back. He was about to deliver some dramatic and abusive remark when the impulse was diverted by an extremely pertinent question which sprang to mind.

"Where did she say I was? During all of this."

"Mr Delaporte, we are talking about a transaction that took but a few minutes on a busy day three months ago. I cannot recall your wife saying you were anywhere in particular. To my recollection she never mentioned you. To be frank, I cannot recall her, or the sale of your house, in any detail at all."

The final insult. Gerry nodded, left the office and closed the door gently behind him. It was the second door he'd closed gently behind him, each time with such consequences, such finality, in less than an hour. As the latch clicked he realized that he still did not know how much she'd sold it for, his house. What did she get for it – his house, the house for which he'd paid the mortgage for more than thirty years? *His* house, his roof, his place in the world. How much? How much for the poky terraced house that had incurred the original debt to which he'd hitched his whole life?

He decided that he did not want to know any more.

Chapter Six

Buckets of tears

There were sounds of feet shuffling and running here and there and of various tools scraping and brushing the surfaces of the floors and walls and doors. There were watery sounds of buckets being filled and of sponges and mops being wrung. And amidst these sounds there was a voice, loud, crisp, authoritative, issuing orders, bellowing sarcasms:

"Oh yes. Very good. Very clever. Now do it again!"

There was the occasional antique insult:

"Where on earth have you been, you filthy ragamuffin?"

"Get on with it, you lazy tyke!"

Gerry even heard someone called a "golliwog", as he slowly climbed his stairs. All this could of course have been humorous, but it clearly was neither meant nor received in that spirit. There was no response to the tyrannical barking but the clanking of buckets and the wringing of mops. Such was the depth of Gerry's depression that he found himself glad to hear the voice of Alec Webb, for surely the emptiness of Claremont Villas would have been the worst homecoming imaginable. Gerry was curious to know who it was that Webb could speak to so overbearingly. Fellow workers in the Cooperative, lowly citizens though they were, surely could not be treated in such a fashion.

"Attention!"

But perhaps they could, because now he was arrested on the stairs by another, different sound. All buckets and mops were at ease and the silence was broken by a steady, even smacking. Blow after blow. Regular, human blows. To the body. And each blow was followed by a muffled, adult moan. After six blows, six of the best, Webb spoke out, his voice very stern indeed:

"You won't do it again, will you, Jake? . . . Will you?"

"No, sir."

"You'll leave the order book alone, won't you, Jake? No more foolery."

"No, sir."

"Now bend over for another six."

"Must I?"

"You know you must."

Another six, measured blows. The final ones drawn out, and their muffled moans much louder, uninhibited.

"*Now get out of my sight!*"

Gerry drew himself in against the banister as Jake came down the stairs. He was a very short man, not much taller than a child, in an old brown polo neck and jeans, with his long hair tied back in a ponytail. Mid-thirties, perhaps. He glanced at Gerry in passing and Gerry looked into his eyes, under the dim stair light. Small, insomniac eyes, in whorls of down. Quite free of excitement, or any other emotion, come to that. Quite shameless eyes. Gerry watched as Jake descended the broken treads to the hallway. At the doorway he shrugged, as if he wore a heavy coat he wanted to settle on his shoulders, before stepping out into the November evening.

What on earth was going on here?

Gerry continued up the stairs.

Children. Quite small children. Four or five boys, no girls, all about ten or eleven years old. Gerry stood on the second floor landing and watched them scuttling from room to room, labouring with such intensity they might have been in a Dickensian workhouse. Webb himself was out of sight in his Office, where the majority of the labourers seemed to be employed. The children were dressed for the work, in dirty t-shirts and worn out jeans. Despite their thin clothes and the chill of the early evening, they were sweating quite profusely. Gerry stood with his Harris Tweed done up at all three buttons, the collar stiff against his neck.

"You bloody nincompoop! You'll have to do that again!"

A small child of mixed race emerged from Webb's Office carrying a brand new steel bucket. His face was dammed tight against tears of anger and humiliation. He walked round Gerry without looking at him and went to the communal toilet at the end of the landing to fetch more water. Gerry followed him with his eyes, watched him crash the bucket into the ancient cast-iron bath, and turn both taps full on. The boy filled the bucket to the brim, but then had to tip half the water out again before he could lift it and carry it back to the Office. Gerry stepped aside to let the struggling child by.

He found his sympathy for him checked by vindictiveness. Some of his worst tormentors, particularly towards the end of his career, had been boys not much older than this. The youngest in his school. Little animals from the council estates whose sensibilities had known no conditioning, whose hysteria and recklessness knew no bounds once the leash was off. The leash? As if he'd ever had a leash! Boys who, in a challenge among themselves of which they could never tire, remained standing on their desks from one bell to the next. Or who began a lesson in a perfectly quiet and proper manner, never said a word or made a sound, did exactly what was required of them, for twenty or even thirty minutes, beavering away – they might even recite some irregular verbs, in a higgledy-piggledy manner! - but then, upon a signal Gerry had never been able to detect, just ten minutes or so from the end of the lesson, when his nerves were taut as bow strings, they had showed him who was boss. Oh, yes. The irregular verbs, the Vocab. Books, were tossed aside and different declensions were offered instead - *Delashit! Delatit! Delaprick!* – amid shrieks, howls of delight, desks banging, feet stamping, rulers slapping and all the bloody rest of it.

The pleasure principle.

The bloody rabblement. The underclass. The great unwashed.

Back at the Office doorway the boy had to circumvent a tall, greatcoated figure.

"Quickly boy! Quickly! You dunderhead!"

This mysterious scene was a short-lived distraction to Gerry's mood. This and the Jake business. Explanations or justifications were of no interest to him. These children – he didn't care where they came from. The furious, miserable energy here, in this dim, echoey, dilapidated corridor, had a psychological resonance for Gerry that shook the crooked props of his mind. Today he had suffered nothing less than an implosion of the personality, and the ensuing vacuum sucked in any trace of invective on the air.

Gerry had always lived with a number of voices in his head, a collection of censorious guests, a bunch of armchair dictators - or rather, hectoring, bullying, badgering teachers, of the kind who'd surrounded him all his life, and whom he'd tried so pitifully to emulate, whose imperious voices had to be served, served, served, who would only keep quiet, only stop talking about him behind his back if he rushed his life away at their behest. And this afternoon he had lost control of those voices. Something had gone missing. He'd lost the little pink Vocab Book in which he'd jotted down all their various demands and commands. He'd lost their lists of rules and tips and hints (*Now Gerry, it's never too late to teach an old dog new tricks . . . Now Gerry, you know as well as I do – Never smile until Easter! . . . Now Gerry, these kids will only parlez-vous with you if you . . .*) and the voices, unassuaged, had grown louder and louder, and some, which he must have forgotten about, which had been asleep in their staff room corners for decades, had been wakened by all the noise, and had joined in the rout of his crumpled ego. This attack of babbling in his head disabled him, wrecked any sequence of thought. The voices declared him useless, feeble, stupid, weak, crass, a maggot, a fool, and now, above these yells and shouts he heard a new voice, more strident than the rest, fresh, young, virile and totally commanding, calling out loud and clear from some new vantage point, by the mantelpiece, perhaps. It was Webb's voice, he had Alec Webb in his head, the old Gordonstounian, bellowing like a bull in a china shop his mad antique insults. Webb commanded him hither and thither and denounced him as a nincompoop, a ragamuffin, a golliwog and a dunderhead.

"Ah, Gerry! I'd begun to wonder where you'd got to. We're having a bit of a spring-clean." Webb approached Gerry. "You all right, old chap? You look all out of it."

Gerry lowered his head and focused on the wet floorboard beneath his feet: the grain, the dirt, that dark, loosened knot.

"Never better."

He looked up, but not at Webb. He folded his arms and frowned at the surrounding activity.

"What is going on here, if you don't mind my asking?"

"*Get a move on!*" Webb shouted at a spindly but spivvy looking boy who was already rushing, his mop out of control and his bucket banging against his shins. Webb was so *loud*. Had Gerry had a voice like that his whole life might have been different. A voice like that, and a leash, and eyes that -

"I thought child labour was a thing of the last century."

Keeping an imperious eye on proceedings, Webb explained. "Head of the local primary is a church friend. He gives me the list of miscreants, I dish out the atonement. Community service, Gerry." He turned on the boy with the bucket again - "I said *scrub* it!" - then looked back at Gerry with knowing, hooded eyes. "Work, you see, Gerry. Work. That's the secret." Webb warmed his hands on the heat of the boys' labour. "No one has given them anything proper to do. No one has put the notion in their pretty heads that in order to survive, they are going to have to work!" Webb abandoned his posturing, and struck a thoughtful note: "I sometimes think a week in the third world would do this lot more good than a year's schooling, you know." He offered Gerry a sideways glance and smiled - some home truths were being ignored, like it or not.

Gerry held the sideways glance.

"And Jake?" he asked.

Webb drew down the corners of his mouth. "Jake?" He looked away. "Jake had some atonement due as well tonight. Justice must be done and must be seen to be done, I'm afraid. Pour encourager les autres."

Gerry said nothing more.

Good grief. All this, still going on, in the nation's capital. How much sweeter it would have been, after all, if the house had been empty. Without even a goodnight to Webb, he turned and went down to his own landing.

His bedroom faced south like the living room next door, but had only the one window. The sash cords were broken and the window was either nailed or had warped itself into its frame. Gerry had been unable to clean away the X from the outside, as he had done with all the living room windows and even the bathroom window. He stopped at the threshold of this cold room with its bare boards and its mattress on the floor. His few spare clothes were draped on one of the wretched kitchen chairs which littered the house. Apart from this chair and the mattress there was no other furniture. For dirty washing there was a cardboard box in one corner, lined with a shopping bag. The street light created a faint shadow of the window's cross that fell over his clothes and ended at his feet. The cross seemed to be pointing at him, as if to say: *Welcome Home!* What a sad room this was. Indeed, it was. Without really thinking about what he was doing, he took a couple of steps further into the room and turned about. He shut his eyes and imagined the condemnatory cross now rested on his back. In fact, it didn't: there was just the blur of one of its members halfway up his Harris Tweed, but he imagined that it fell square on his shoulders and he took a deep breath and held it. He jutted out his jaw and clenched his teeth together hard enough to crack the enamel. He held himself like that, without breathing, without breaking, bearing his cross. After a minute he exhaled and let his frame sag and his clothes hung on his bones as if on a manikin.

Oh my word. What a sad little room this was!

He tipped the kitchen chair so that his spare clothes slipped with a soft thud to the floorboards, and sat himself down. From his inside pocket he removed the bundle of letters he had collected from his home in Rosebery Road, Ipswich. Of course he had been through the bundle before to check there was no farewell letter from Anna and of course there was no such letter. Once safely on the coach he had opened his own letter to her. He had read it to himself for the first time – *and now you have the opportunity to gloat. I swore that would never happen . . . I had to get out there naked and alone . . . We shall return to our original plans. Please call Ebbages -*

Ah yes.

What Gerry had not done so far though was open the other letters, which were all from the same faithful correspondent: Barclaycard International, Liverpool. Fanning the letters at the window he could just make out from their postmarks that they were arranged in the order they had arrived. He opened the bottom one, which was simply a statement which recorded that there had been six separate cash withdrawals from his account on consecutive days, the first date falling immediately after his departure back in August. Each withdrawal had been for the maximum daily allowance: one hundred pounds. The account's credit was used up therefore within the six days, and there were no other transactions recorded on the statement. They had always kept a note of their PINs, written in reverse order, at the bottom of their Bank file, on the inside, in the crease, one marked G, one marked A. Anna's idea.

"You are very particular, Anna."

"Not particular. Sensible. Cautious. One of us has to be."

Gerry had a pretty good idea what lay within the other envelopes, yet he could not resist opening the uppermost one, which had arrived at his home only a few days ago. This letter, terse and clear, stated that legal proceedings were now in progress against him in order to recover the six hundred pounds, plus interest, owed to Barclaycard International. He was also advised that, in the event of the case being upheld, his creditors would be seeking his personal liability for their legal costs.

Gerry sat before the window, the big white letter in his fingers, his hands in his lap, the weak yellow rays of the street light falling across him. What a long day it had been.

And it was in this quiet attitude, sitting on the kitchen chair, the threatening letter in his hand, that Sir Alec Webb discovered him. He knocked softly on the bedroom door, as if anticipating the scene within. When there was no reply he turned the handle and pushed the door back. It creaked open theatrically and came to rest against the corner of Gerry's mattress. Seeing Gerry in his immobile state in the gathering gloom, Sir Alec stopped in the doorway. He looked about the room, took in the whole sorry picture, then retreated to fetch a second chair for himself.

He carried his chair all the way in, careful to make as little noise as possible, and set it a few feet in front of Gerry, who did not move or in any way acknowledge his presence. Gerry stared impassively at the window, at the lurid glow trapped in a thousand flecks and drip marks on the filthy glass.

Sir Alec Webb, having sat back a minute in the expectation that Gerry might turn to him and speak, assumed the initiative. He leant forward and gently squeezed Gerry's knee.

"Come on, ole feller," he said. "Let's have a talk."

Gerry turned to the tall, shadowy figure in the greatcoat. The physical gesture had caught him unawares. No one had made any physical approach to him, no one had deliberately touched any part of his body, except in salutation, for years, too many years. With his concentration, with his whole mind in such disarray, a sympathetic gesture like that, even from a person he despised, affected him. It reached him. It brought words to his throat. It nearly brought sobs.

"Where are the children?"

"Gone. Gone back to their wretched homes and ungoverned lives, Gerry. Poor so-and-sos."

"But you were cruel to them. Cruel to be kind, of course, one presumes."

"With children like that you have to be, Gerry. No other way.

The confidence of this simple judgement made Gerry turn to the window once more. This evening it seemed a wondrous thing to hear someone talk with such conviction, such self-belief. But then, of course, he was a fool.

"What is it Gerry? What's happened? You looked so exhausted upstairs I expected you to be asleep, but here you are."

Gerry turned again. In the monochrome of dusk the unsightliness of Webb's face was hidden. The lips had not their saveloy fullness. The silly fringe was all but invisible. Despite his revulsion for this young man, Gerry was tempted to tell him what had happened. He needed to hear himself say it. Because the hardest thing about Gerry's forty days and forty nights in the wilderness had not been penury or degradation. The hardest thing had been an appalling loneliness. He'd found it astonishingly difficult to get used to this feeling. He had discovered, since leaving home, that far from being two nations, as the papers repeatedly claimed these days, England was perhaps twenty or thirty different nations, or maybe even fifty or sixty, with such subtle distinctions of language and manner separating nation from nation that given any random selection of the populace, such as existed here, at Claremont Villas, or such as had existed in the hostel in Paddington, for example, no two people could communicate with each other, even if they felt inclined to do so. In fact, at that hostel a rude anti-sociability, at least as far as Gerry was concerned, had been the one genuinely national characteristic. From the moment of his arrival, as soon as the other inmates had heard how he spoke, Gerry had found himself set apart. On the other beds there had been a general turning of shoulders towards the wall. These people never knew what a disservice they did Gerry during this period. Had he found himself accepted, wanted, useful, he would have been content to stay put in the hostel for heaven knows how long. The truth was he had cherished some quite romantic notions of that way of life. He had imagined visits to a local cafe where time was passed swapping anecdotes of broken lives, while nursing cups of weak but spiritually nourishing tea, served, with the occasional bacon sandwich perhaps, by a humane and tolerant cafe proprietor, called Frank or Alf - a thoroughbred, big-hearted cockney. Frank or Alf would also lend Gerry and his friends the cafe's scruffy game of chess, or dominoes, to while away an idle hour. Over their shoulders, as he served the tea and bacon sandwiches, he'd take an interest in the game, but be too shy or too busy to play himself. He'd bring them extra pots of tea for nothing so that he could keep up with who was winning –

On the house, gents . . .

But at the hostel in Westbourne Grove life hadn't been quite like that. There had been no camaraderie whatever, no local cafe. His fellow inmates had all been far too young for that reflective and philosophical way of life. Some were young enough to be his grandchildren. These young men had not been interested in conversation, chess, or even dominoes. Instead they gambled. They smoked, and drank, and they gambled. They played pontoon or brag incessantly, recklessly, drunkenly, stupidly. The same few pounds changed hands day by day, night by night. They craved distraction from the huge lives looming out there on the street, all the time, and hanging over them indoors, shapeless as the blue smoke above the card game. Rather than an atmosphere of collective commiseration, such as Gerry had looked forward to, there had been an atmosphere of competitive individualism in the hostel. The mad gambling broke up any tentative allegiance and aggravated natural divisions. The young men cursed and fought and cried out over pontoon and brag, over bad debts and bum deals - *Twist! Burn! Bust! . . . Hey cunt! What, fucker? Take that, cunt!* A passion for fair play ran fierce in these homeless young men, fierce as their hormones. From where they'd sunk to, the idea of having a run of bad luck was inconceivable. They ignored Gerry's explanations about probability, his moral twitterings from the sidelines, his gentle bedside counsel to the losers. To those losers Gerry offered – still keen to swap stories - analogies from his own experience as a young man, when he'd lost on the turf at Newmarket or Market Rasen. He sat on the bedside with his knee clasped between his hands, recounting his ancient, irrelevant memories. It was the closest he came to that fantasy hostel lifestyle, to the swapping of anecdotes from broken lives. *So, don't you see? One man's profit is another man's loss, you know, and your turn will come around too in the fullness of time, don't worry. Oh yes it will . . . Whether one bets on the bob-tail or the bay, you see, it all comes around . . . Swings and roundabouts, you see . . .* He was ignored. It wasn't a question of bad luck or good luck to these young gamblers. Theirs was a closed world of cheats and conspiracies. Cheats were everywhere, all around them. And indeed they were. Fights broke out. The young men punched and lashed out at each other. Some had knives or homemade clubs, hidden from the wardens, weapons they'd hung on to from their nights sleeping out in cardboard boxes.

Gerry had still found it in his heart to pity these young men, even though he was universally rejected by them. Youth itself had become such an overshadowing anxiety. The best years of health and hormones were slipping by before their very eyes. No such generous sentiments had been returned to Gerry, though. One of his moments of bitterest disillusionment at the hostel came towards the end of his stay, when he overheard, just as he approached the dormitory, a young Scot, a clever youth for whom he'd bought a drink on more than one occasion, mention him in passing. The Scot, slouched in the doorway with his back to Gerry, was in conversation with someone on a bed behind the door -

"Oh ay," he was saying. "But didee rreelly say thaat? Rreelly? The Bof? Did he rreelly say thaat? . . . "

Some witticism came from behind the door, because the Scot threw his head back and laughed out loud.

Prof, a title one of the more amiable wardens had given

Gerry, was, as Gerry liked to put it, his *"accustomed sobriquet"*.

But the Scot had not called him *Prof.* He had called him Bof. It was quite unmistakable.

Boring Old Fart.

Such memories were best set aside. Too painful. And yet, when all was said and done, prospects had been better then, three months ago, than they were this evening in Claremont Villas, in this desperate room. When Gerry looked up at Webb he wore a smile full of long-suffering, of quiet despair.

"I have lost everything I own," he said. "All that I had. My house, its furnishings, my money, my savings. Even my credit on my credit card. All of it. Everything I had worked for. All my life. Strived for. Sacrificed for. All of it is gone now. Quite gone." He shook his head. "I am ruined."

In the poor light it was all but imperceptible, but Sir Alec raised an eyebrow at that last adjective.

"That's hard, Gerry."

"It was my wife, you see. My wife. She took everything I had. Sold everything and took all of my money. Stole everything. You see?"

"What, for herself?"

"Of course."

"Herself alone?"

Gerry turned to the window, to its lurid drips and flecks.

Oh my word. Oh my God! The explosive thought that she had taken it all for the benefit of someone else! - My God! - *some other man!* - taken all his money, his pension, his savings, his credit, to be spent on some other man, who, even now, was sitting with her, lying with her, laughing with her somewhere, sitting in a pub with her, drinking a manly pint with her, and throwing his head back and laughing out loud with her, or sharing fish & chips with her somewhere, on Brighton Pier, on Whitstable beach, on Weymouth sea front - these giddy, maddening ideas, only occurred to Gerry with Webb's blundering prompt. But now he could see them so clearly – Anna and someone else! They were walking arm in arm eating fish & chips on the stony beach! He could see them, their linked arms, and Anna turning and smiling and laughing, pulling the man closer to her. He could see her dyed auburn hair caught in the wind. He could see them from where he drowned far out at sea, drowned under useless waves of emotion. Gerry struggled to fend off Webb's idea as if it were a sea mine, a huge black mine breaking the briny surface, something forgotten from the war, covered in barnacles and rusty spikes – He could not keep it at bay!

He would be blown to smithereens!

He swallowed, though his mouth was dry. With anxious, fluttering fingers he folded up the Barclaycard letter and put it away in the inside pocket of his Harris Tweed.

"But you can find her, surely, and bring the matter to rights?" Sir Alec continued reasonably. "You must have some idea where she would have gone, or where they might have gone."

Gerry forced his concentration onto the former option.

"She had only one relative alive. An older sister. A spinster. They didn't get on. They hadn't seen each other in years."

"Ah . . . All the more likely, then, Gerry."

"What?"

"Some new *compagnon*. Cherchez l'homme, Gerry."

"Now look here - " Gerry held up a hand, but he could not remonstrate, just could not do it.

He dropped his hand and looked to the window again, as if the yellow light offered a way out, an escape from all this. But escape to where? Out there? A car sped by down Lonsdale Road, and then another came along more slowly and drew to a halt. Doors slammed. No voices. No footsteps. Not that he could hear . . .

Linking arms. The stony beach. Someone else. *Some other man!* Gerry hung his head. *Some new compagnon!*

"If she went abroad there's a chance the police . . . the police could trace her passport." But then he added with sudden conviction, shaking his head firmly: "She would not have gone abroad, though. Never. Never in a thousand years."

"Ah, but Gerry - "

"What?"

"With someone new, Gerry, you see." Webb leant forward. "Don't you see it? That's different, then, isn't it? Don't you see? This other feller could have talked her into it. You know, some ne'er-do-well, some unscrupulous feller, some smooth talker. Or some lush, you know. Some bounty-hunting type."

Gerry wrung his hands.

A ne'er-do-well. A *lush.* A *bounty-hunting* type. A blarneying Irishman. A canny Scot. A windbag Taff. A foul-mouthed Scouse. A roughneck Geordie. Younger than her. Motoring down to Provence in an open-top car. He drives, of course. An extempore tour through Limoges, perhaps, why not, through Clermont-Ferrand and Saint-Etienne. He had always promised her that. How often he had promised her that - an open-top car - and promised *himself* too. Promised her Clermont and now he lived in Claremont!

His mind reeled in pain, kicked back on itself, reeled again -

Some lush, some bounty-hunting type, with his money, his savings, his life savings, every stick of furniture sold, every stick, oh yes, to beat him with - Jake, oh Jake - Barclaycard, open-top car, compagnon, Clermont-Ferrand, Barclaycard, Claremont, Jake, fish & chips, stony beach, open-top car -

- Fill her up, garçon! There's a good chap! Go on! Doesn't matter! Gerry's paying! Gerry's paying for everything! Gerry will pay! Gerry will pay! -

"You must have some idea where you might begin looking, Gerry. The police can circulate photographs of missing persons, of course."

Circulate them in Clermont, Claremont, Limoges -

"I have no photographs."

"Not one?"

"None."

"Forgive me, Gerry, but your wife does sound extraordinarily resourceful. And of course, if she's been picked up by - Oh! - wait a minute, if she herself - "

"ENOUGH! . . ."

A respectful silence followed.

Gerry hung his head. After a few moments he began muttering to the floor, not really talking to Webb at all. "I imagine she expects - she expects me to do away with myself somehow - she expects - as a duty – that's it – a duty, a *duty* - thus solving any remaining problems. She'd collect - she expects, she collects - tidy sum in life assurance - very tidy sum - "

"Now Gerry," Sir Alec interrupted, drawing himself up, "we'll have no talk of that kind."

With this counsel Webb's presence became utterly intolerable. This avuncular posturing from one so young – as if Gerry knew nothing of life, had learned nothing from kicking around down here for more than half a century! – this was really quite beyond the pale. But then, really, when you got down to it, what did he know about life?

What had he actually learned about life? He'd spent it in a classroom, for goodness' sake! What? That's real life? What could you learn about life if you just sat in the classroom for fifty years? Never ventured outside it. Could he, should he, sit here, on this kitchen chair, in this wretched room in Claremont Villas, and claim to have had 'a life'? It seemed like glamorizing everything to call all this piffling misery 'life'.

Gerry looked Webb in the face. The corners of his mouth turned down grimly. "I think you had better go now," he said. "I really do."

"Not just yet, Gerry. I shall go, certainly, have no fear, but not just yet."

"Go now. Get out."

"You're in no fit state for your own company, Gerry."

Gerry let out a long, stale sigh to the floor. What an affliction this young man was. This upper class fool. This Christian pup.

"Gerry, I need to remind you about a couple of things," Sir Alec said, and he leant towards Gerry's humped and diminished figure. "I need to remind you that we all do at least one very terrible thing in our lives, for which it is possible we cannot be forgiven by those we love. It is beyond them. Maybe Anna, your wife, whom you loved for many years, and whom, I suspect, you still cannot find it in your heart to hate, maybe she has now done such a thing to you. Maybe. Maybe."

Gerry scowled and shook his head at the floor. This awful young man. This ghastly young man. Such a torment. A demon from hell itself.

"The second thing I need to remind you about is that your life is not your own to dispose of as you please. Oh no. That would be too easy. There have been many times when I would only too gladly have taken that way out. But

I had no right. You have no right. I had to resist, I had to go on."

Gerry looked up squarely now at the speaker of these lines, in the deepening gloom.

"You should not have done that, you know," he said.

Webb looked at him askance.

"You should not have gone on, you see." Gerry sat up and straightened his back, arched his back, trying to brace himself, divert himself with this personal attack. "There's your mistake, you see. The error of your ways. You should not have done that. Carried on. Gone on. You should have called it a day. You should have let some other poor creature have your bread and water. Some starving soul in Africa, perhaps. That could have been arranged, you know, these days, very easily. Just think. If you'd only made some arrangements, then done away with yourself, topped yourself, a host of starving souls in Africa, in Ethiopia or Chad, or in Angola or Mozambique, could have lived and thrived – could have had a chance in life - could have had a chance *of* life! - but for you and your Christian selfishness. You are a murderer. That is what you are. You are nothing but a worthless, selfish, common murderer."

There was a pause. Webb shook his head slowly. It was impossible to see his bald eyes now but Gerry sensed the wise, hooded look behind the glasses.

"Gerry, you are overwrought. You really have no idea what you're saying."

Gerry drew in a deep breath. He exhaled then took in another, deeper breath. He bellowed at Alec Webb, as he had heard Webb bellow half an hour before at the miscreant children -

"*GET OUT! GET OUT! GET OUT!*"

He sat back, breathless, and with the last of his strength gestured to the door. "Get out. Go away. You are an idiot."

Still Sir Alec did not move. He knitted his hands behind his neck and sighed patiently.

"Fuck off," said Gerry. "Go on. Fuck off."

"Now, why use language like that, Gerry?"

For a full minute Gerry did not know what to do. There was no getting rid of the man. Then he stood up, patted his jacket pocket for his keys, turned, and shuffled out of the room. Once outside he unlocked the door to his living room, slipped in and had just got the key into the lock when he felt the pressure of Webb the other side. With a final shove he pushed the door home and wrenched round the key.

"Gerry? . . . Gerry . . . If you need me I'll be right outside."

Chapter Seven

New Tenancies

Kim and Mik were two young lovers down on their luck. Prospects were not good: neither had a job, and neither had any formal qualifications of any kind. However, Kim had been told by an older, wiser friend, with whom she'd shared a house in Holloway, that she had artistic talent, and that she should go to Art School. This breath of encouragement had given just enough life to the future for Kim to enjoy the present. Mik didn't have any artistic talent, but he didn't worry about the future either.

Taken in by Kim's teenage prettiness, Sir Alec had told the couple they could join Two Strong Arms as a pair of mural painters, Mik taking the rôle of Kim's assistant. Sir Alec sensed a shiftiness about Mik, a laziness, and outlined in some detail what he had in mind here. To start with Mik would have to prepare the walls they were going to paint - he would scrub the bricks and re-point the mortar, make good any woodwork, mark out the mural; in addition he would mix the paint, carry the paint-pots, clean the tools and brushes, and sweep up afterwards. Sir Alec drew up quite a list of useful jobs that Mik could do, while smiling now and then at his artistic partner. But at the moment all of those jobs Sir Alec had specified, all those mucky trowels and buckets and mortar boards, the stacks of paint-pots and dirty brushes, all of it lay in a heap just around the corner: it was all in the future, and Mik didn't worry about the future.

Kim and Mik were very much indebted to Sir Alec Webb and listened to him attentively and treated him with due respect. He had solved their current housing difficulties. He had invited them to move into Two Strong Arms' new premises on the second floor of Claremont Villas. They had taken up residence in the rooms previously designated as the Interview Room and the Waiting Room. They hadn't done any work for the Cooperative yet, but after much toing and froing they had managed to get their social security payments delivered to the new address, so money was no tighter than it had always been.

Gerry was not around on December 1st, the day they moved in. He was pursuing various details about his wife's disappearance at the police station in Ladbroke Road. It had been a long and very wearing day for Gerry Delaporte. His case was not proceeding smoothly. His first contact with the police nearly three weeks ago had started things off on the wrong foot. He'd discovered that established procedure in a case such as his began with apathy, progressed to inertia, and concluded with blithe indifference. As far as the police were concerned it was a domestic dispute and their hands were tied. It's a domestic, you see, sir, and that's that. Plaintiff can take what steps he likes to find his wife, and good luck to him. Best of

British. Gerry had been nonplussed by this attitude but not defeated. What of the sale of his home and property, the theft of his commuted pension and his pension to date? Surely there was a case to be answered there, was there not? He remained calm and rational and insistent. With some reluctance the desk sergeant had conceded that there might be (if such allegations could be substantiated), and in the end Gerry had been invited behind the desk to have an interview with a C.I.D. officer. A Detective Sergeant, no less. D.S.Tenmere. The buck, it seemed, had successfully been passed. But it was at this point that matters became particularly trying, for all concerned, because Gerry had no documentary evidence about his person, nor in his possession at Claremont Villas, to corroborate his story. Nothing at all. How shrewd Anna had been, he realized. And how incredibly naive, how trusting, how stupid he had been. It was only after he had persuaded the C.I.D. officer to make contact with Maidment & Co., Solicitors, and Ebbages Estate Agents in Ipswich, that the police began to take him at all seriously. From here things started to move, but oh so slowly. It was another week before charges for the unlawful appropriation and disposal of Gerry's property and assets were finally drawn up against Mrs Anna Delaporte, formerly of 13 Rosebery Road, Ipswich. And then how was she to be traced? Having set out the charges the police appeared to lose interest, their job was done. They simply had to wait until Anna turned herself in. On the other hand Gerry expected nothing less than a nationwide search, with posters at every bus-stop and railway platform. But no. An identikit picture would be made up, and the search would be restricted to just a handful of places at a time, where the picture would be displayed inside or outside the main police station. That was it. Nothing more than that. Gerry knew well the kind of publicity they had in mind here. The implausible black and white jigsaw sketch, weathering in a leaky wooden frame, seen only by those with police business, whose minds were generally on other things than the disappearance of a retired schoolmaster's wife some months ago. Wasn't any police officer actually going to venture out into the cold and rain and look for Anna Delaporte? No. Absolutely not. The police would act only on information brought to their attention by members of the public. On this point Detective Sergeant Tenmere was categorical, and Gerry sensed further protest would prove counter-productive.

He was consulted for his views about where his wife might have gone, and, despite a growing despair with the whole business, did at last feel he was of some use. Of two things he was pretty sure. Anna would definitely have moved to the coast. She loved the sea and the seaside. And she would have gone south. Not north in a month of Sundays. Bath, Bristol, Bournemouth. These were her kinds of places.

But on the afternoon of December 1st, for the second time, the identikit picture drawn up by the C.I.D. bore not the slightest resemblance to his wife. The picture was really quite absurd. He told them so. He said it was ridiculous. A child could have done better. And having rejected the proffered sketch and scorned, in passing, the abilities of the police artist concerned - *A graduate of The Royal Academy, did you say?* - he found himself once again under suspicion of being a time-wasting vagrant.

So on his return to Claremont Villas he was in a state of some agitation, and in dire need of the toilet too. After relieving himself he went to his bedroom to lie down and gather his wits about him, but discovered straightaway this new problem to deal with, this new challenge, this new invasion of his privacy. He'd no sooner shut his bedroom room door than he heard the sound of heavy shoes coming down the stairs from the floor above, and more than one pair. It did not sound like Webb and crazily, having just returned from the Police Station, he thought of the footsteps of various constables going ponderously about their business. He had to investigate. Perhaps the police were looking for Alec Webb themselves, for breaking and entering; perhaps the long arm of the law was about to grapple with Two Strong Arms; maybe this was a chance to shop Webb and undo him. The sense had never left Gerry that this was his house, even though Webb had now installed himself in the Office above, that now had a desk and telephone (as yet unconnected). Gerald was accountable for this property to the Greater London Council and the dreaded Red Ken Livingstone; in a filing cabinet in the bowels of some municipal bunker his name was in their records and sooner or later, when they finally called in the contractors to demolish or refurbish the house, his file would be taken out and dusted down and he would be contacted. At which stage he would be *offered alternative accommodation.* Gerry knew well that point of the housing law, but he remained anxious that in some way Alec Webb's subcultural activities might jeopardize his delicate position by false association. He would do anything he could to shop Webb, to get him out, evict him from Claremont Villas.

In this wild and distracted state, full of treacherous lies and allegations, Gerry stepped out onto his landing to challenge and attack, like the ugly troll in the storybook:

Who's that trip-trapping over my bridge?

But he stopped dead outside his bedroom doorway.

Here were Mik and Kim, two young people he had never seen before in his life. They had just reached his landing.

Kim had long brown hair and an open, pretty face, though her brows were a little heavy, perhaps. No make-up at all. Her complexion was so fresh Gerry thought she could be no more than sixteen. She wore a scruffy fur coat that made her look older, but not much. She smiled immediately on seeing Gerry and this smile, taking Gerry by complete surprise, provoked within him a flush of shame. He looked down a moment and took in her tight jeans, and the bright yellow clogs on her bare feet, in December.

It was her simple courtesy, her open good-nature which embarrassed him. Since his trip to Ipswich Gerry had let things go again. Several days' silvery growth adorned his chin, and beneath the stubble his face was dirty from the filthy air of the street, in which he spent so much time on his blind and pointless walks. His clothes were baggy and unwashed. He knew he fitted the rôle in which the police had tried to cast him today – time-wasting vagrant. And because that is how he looked, that is how he was treated. He could surely expect no more than to be dealt with brusquely by shopkeepers, policemen and all officialdom, and contemptuously by perfect strangers. Yet this attractive young girl had taken no notice of his appearance at all. To her he was not an angry troll. She had looked into his eyes and she had smiled.

The young man, Mik, was older by two or three years at least. He might have been in his early twenties. His features were rather blunt and unappealing but there was a docility about him which had a charm of its own for Gerry, accustomed as he was to young males being rude and obstreperous.

Mik stood back from his girlfriend, as if used to letting her take the lead in things.

"Excuse me," Gerry began, closing his bedroom door behind him, shutting off his shameful quarters, "but I don't believe we've been introduced." He offered this in his fruitiest tones, attempting at once to establish his education and at the same time, with a wry smile and a cock of his learned head, to acknowledge its worthlessness in the present circumstances.

"I'm Kim," the girl said. She turned to Mik, who had stiffened slightly at Gerry's first utterance, his first salvo, "And this is Mik."

Gerry nodded to the young man, then turned back to Kim.

"I don't wish to seem presumptuous, and do please pardon my curiosity," he began again, wringing his hands, drawing this out for all it was worth, which really was not very much, and he knew it, "but would you please explain to me, if you would be so kind, exactly what you are doing in my house?"

A maidenly flush came to the girl's cheek. Gerry delighted in drawing first blood.

Mik said: "We live here."

Gerry turned on the young man, his movement quick, his eyelids fluttering.

"Oh, so you're persona grata here too, are you?"

"If you like."

"Well I don't like, I'm afraid. I am the landlord here. And I know nothing of any new tenancies."

"Mr Webb said - "

"Forget Mr Webb. He is not the landlord here. I am. Mr Webb is a tenant of mine. In fact, I am in the process right now of evicting Mr Webb."

"Evicting him?" Mik scowled. "On what grounds?"

"On the grounds, sir," Gerry proceeded, eyelids fluttering wildly now, "that he is a first-class, pedigree arsehole. I don't need any other grounds. I am the landlord here."

This assault on Alec Webb, who had offered them work as mural painters, who had solved their current housing difficulties, was clearly shocking, particularly to the girl.

"I'm sorry," she said, "but I don't think you have any right to talk about Mr Webb like that, even if you don't get on." Her voice indicated some education in her own background, but there was no accent Gerry could get hold of.

"Come on," Mik said, turning to the stairs. "Come on. Forget about it."

Kim turned to follow.

"I repeat! I am the landlord!" Gerry called after them. He approached the head of the stairs and clutched the banister. They were picking their way down between the broken treads. "If Mr Webb has sublet any rooms to you, the rent is due to me!"

Mik hesitated at the foot of the stairs and looked back up at Gerry. "If you're the landlord," he said reasonably, "when're you going to do something about these stairs? They're dangerous."

Gerry glowered down at the pair of them, then pulled back, still clutching the banister, as if about to launch forward again and bellow down some final riposte, or even spit on them. The young man muttered something to his girlfriend, something about Mr Webb, and then flicked a parting glance up at Gerry, unimpressed by the latter's overbearing attitude. They left without another word. As soon as the front door drew to, which was all it did now, there had been no lock or latch of any kind since Webb had jemmied his way in, Gerry started up the stairs to the second floor. He was going to find out just what had been going on behind his back.

He had not ventured up here since the afternoon of his return from Ipswich. The child slaves, for all Webb's bullying, had not accomplished much. Across the floors and windows and walls were broad swathes of washed dirt. The dust had simply been liquefied, spread about in huge swirling patterns, and then left to dry. The effect was oddly pleasing, but the curls and swirls were already scuffed away in many places. Gerry took a look around, muttering to himself, thinking of Mik and Kim, and Alec Webb, and Two Strong Arms, and cursing the whole futile and idiotic enterprise. He stared at the filthy swipes across the window of Webb's Office. Why on earth didn't Webb spend five minutes on the windows himself? The lazy toff! It was surely worth it. The views were really very pleasant from up here, out towards Arundel Gardens and Ladbroke Gardens. Gerry turned away and came to the Interview Room. The Interview Room, indeed! Such pretence! It was ludicrous. It was pathetic. That silly word was right for once.

No doorhandle. He pushed the door back gently. Inside there was a mattress on the floor. It had sheets and blankets and was neatly made up. This, of course, was the critical piece of furniture for young people of this kind, Gerry reflected, for the Kims and Miks of the world, the quims and pricks of the world. Something to fuck on. He looked about irritably. There was a strange shelving arrangement against the other wall. It comprised a series of wooden slats of various kinds, melamine shelves, slices of blockboard, chipboard, floorboards, all supported by pairs of milk bottles at either end. Gerry frowned at the structure. There were forty or so milk bottles altogether, including a huddle of spares tucked to one side. What would the Milk Marketing Board have to say about this, hmmn? Gerry stared at the shelves. He had not seen anything of this description before and he had to admit to being impressed by the ingenuity of the piece. Milk bottles. They had all been thoroughly cleaned of course, otherwise the place would stink. But actually the room smelt rather pleasant. Gerry opened his nostrils wide and inhaled. Incense. He couldn't see where it came from, but it was really very agreeable. Rather better than the cooking smells, the eggy smells, the toast and beans smells, the bodily odours that pervaded his own pit downstairs. With that troubling comparison Gerry moved on to the next room. Again there was no doorhandle for this room. The absence of doorhandles had been one of the things that had decided Gerry against the rooms on this floor when he'd first arrived. That and the stairs. He stopped and hung his head and shut his eyes at the recollection. To have such firm memories of this place now. The months were passing. It was December. Very soon it would be Christmas. That was an imponderable. Four months since the end of the summer term in July, since the absurd speeches ("*Gerry's a gentleman and we all love him dearly, and we shall all miss him a great deal, and we shall all always remember him*") and the laughter just beneath the applause, and the cheap gift, a self-assembly standard lamp from Texas Homecare. *("Under which, at eventide, Gerry might like to recollect some of the many joys of his long career*") Four months since the drive home for the last time through the familiar Ipswich streets. It had been hot, even in the late afternoon. The town centre streets had been full of knots of young girls improperly dressed. The Friday afternoon sun had lifted their spirits, lifted their skirts, had brought out sudden exposures of flesh all over the place. Bare thighs, bare midriffs, bare arms. Denim shorts frayed at the buttocks - youth, flesh, gaiety. High street doors were wedged open and music spilled onto the pavement. It had been during that late afternoon drive through Ipswich town centre, after the speeches, with a few glasses of inferior red wine inside him, in the sun, in the heat, in the stuffy car, that Gerry had begun to feel the first stirrings of depression. Real depression. Nothing like what he'd known before, not the plain, familiar, grinding misery he'd put up with for thirty years. Not that. Real depression. The first stretchings and tearings asunder of whatever ligaments suspended his soul, and beneath that the blackness, the bottomless sense of waste and worthlessness, and the grave yawning open under him.

Ah well.

He pressed on. In this second room there was another bed, but nothing else. Another bed? Did that mean another tenant? The bed was made up in the same tidy way as the first. Again there was a scent in the room, stronger here. Gerry noted another milk bottle with a few incense sticks in the corner. The room was clean, hospitable, ready for use. There was no other furniture and there was nothing on the walls. Gerry had expected gaudy posters of pop stars or film stars. He was obscurely disappointed not to find any. This couple was proving difficult to typify.

Suddenly he stiffened.

There were steps on the stairs, voices.

He hadn't time to return to his own rooms. In a moment of panic he thought of going up to the third floor, but it was too late. He listened hard. To his relief he heard that the voices were both male. One was unmistakable. It was Alec Webb's voice. Gerry strained his ears. He expected the other to be Mik's. They had come back to sort things out with him after the little contretemps on the landing. Get physical, perhaps. Four strong arms. But it was not Mik's voice. It was a London voice, and young, which he recognized but couldn't quite place.

He decided to brazen it out. He was the de facto landlord and he had a legitimate right to be snooping around up here. Things were taking place without consultation. He was being bypassed and he would let Alec Webb know – and anyone else who needed to know - that that was not on.

Webb reached the second floor landing first, a little puffed out, and was followed by the lean young man Gerry had met about a month ago: Mr Fitzroy, the carpenter who had come for one of Webb's 'interviews'. Gerry remembered him but he looked different now. He wore the same jean suit but it was not so clean and blue as it had been before. For his last interview it might even have been pressed. Most sadly his new baseball boots, which had made him look so fleet of foot, were now scuffed and worn and had even burst in places about the toe. The tigerish laces were reduced to shaggy grey moustaches, no trace of dye remaining. Things had not been working out too well for this young man. He looked wary and unsmiling and he kept both his hands tucked up to the knuckle in the tight pockets of his jeans.

"Hi there, Gerry," Webb said, strolling by, leading the way to his Office.

Mr Fitzroy nodded acknowledgement at Gerry but said nothing. His face was taut and drawn. Gerry remembered the cocky smile of their previous encounter. Things had changed all right. This fellow was feeling the pinch of these straitened times. He wondered if he should inform the lad of what his distinguished name meant. Fitzroy: bastard son of a king. Perhaps this was not quite the moment. Fitzroy was chewing very hard, mercilessly gnawing away at the flesh of his lean cheek.

Gerry watched them enter the Office. Webb sidled round

to his chair behind the desk.

"It's like I said downstairs," Mr Fitzroy began, as he closed the door behind him. "Maybe we got off on the wrong foot. I really am very interested in the project. The Cooperative. Two Strong Arms, wasn't it?"

Gerry decided to hang around for this.

"John," Webb said. "You won't fool me, and you'd be singularly ill-advised to try to fool yourself. Come on. You need work. You're broke. The kitty's dry. That's why you're here, and for no other reason."

"I need work," John Fitzroy conceded. "You're right, Mr Webb. You're dead right. No point in messing around. Whatever you've got, Mr Webb, sir."

"Hold on there . . ."

Gerry could imagine Webb now undoing his coat and sitting back more expansively, taking control of the interview now this young man had put himself in the position of supplicant. Gerry moved a couple of steps closer. Fitzroy's voice had died a little behind the door.

"Hold on there a minute, John. It's not so cut and dried. Not yet. I need to ask a few questions."

"Sure. Fire away. Anything you like."

"My first question is this. It may take you a little by surprise, but bear with me. All will become clear. Here's the first question."

For a few moments no one said anything, at least nothing that was audible. Gerry began to wonder if he'd missed something. Were Webb's questions written down? Cue cards?

"I'm sorry," Fitzroy said at last. "Have I missed it?"

"No," Webb replied, in his leisurely drawl. Gerry could imagine the patronizing smile on his ripe lips. "No, John. You haven't missed anything. Not yet. I just wanted to be sure I had your undivided attention. Here's the first question."

Again a pause. What games!

"Yes?"

"Do you know, John," Webb's voice was measured out in grams. "Do you know what a parable is?"

There was no answer to this question, but Fitzroy must have made some gesture signifying ignorance.

"Right," Webb began. "A parable is a story, a simple story, such as we find in the New Testament, which has some parallel - parable, parallel - with our own lives, and which can teach us to see our actions in a particular light. By the bye, Joseph was a carpenter, you know. Did you know that?"

Again Fitzroy said nothing, but he must have gestured an affirmative reply this time.

"Good. Don't worry," Webb said. "I'm not going to read you anything from the Holy Book! I just wanted to refresh your memory. I'm sure you must have heard this one at school. The parable of the three vineyards. Do you know it?"

"Sure."

"You do? Good. Jolly good. Tell it to me, John."

There was a pause before Fitzroy responded. "Isn't that the one . . ." Fitzroy said something else which Gerry couldn't catch, and to which there was no answer from his interviewer. Then he asked if Webb minded if he smoked.

"I do, but go ahead," Webb replied. "Can you tell it to me, John?"

"What?"

"Tell me the parable of the three vineyards, if you please."

There was a click of a lighter, an audible inhalation, then: "He turns the water into wine?" Fitzroy seemed to have made a decision in lighting his cigarette, a decision to stay calm, play ball, say whatever was necessary.

"Aha! No. No no no," Webb corrected. "He does that at a certain wedding. That was the first miracle. The wedding at Cana in Galilee. Water into wine. Do you know that one?"

"Sure."

"Jolly good. Tell it to me, John."

There was another deep inhalation on the cigarette and a more lengthy pause before Fitzroy replied: "Look, Mr Webb, how about letting me have a look at that order book, and let's see what's what, eh? Eh? What d'you say? I swear I'll take anything. I'll fit cat-flaps. That's fine. I'll fit bog-seats, if you like. I'll do anything. Just let's have a look, see what's what. What d'you say?"

Gerry could smell suddenly the scent of Fitzroy's tobacco from within. He found the smell objectionable but it couldn't move him from his place at the door. Webb, ignoring his interviewee's rather desperate plea, was suddenly in full swing:

"There was once a very rich owner of vineyards, John," he began. Pleasure swelled his voice. There was an audible relish, a delight in the rôle of moral storyteller. The pastor. "And one day some labourers, who had travelled far and who'd had, so they thought, a pretty tough time of it, approached his door seeking to sell their labour. The rich man was not unkind. He took pity on these men and put them to work in the first of his three vineyards. Then a little later in the day a second group of labourers came to his door. 'Oh master', they said - "

Gerry now stood immediately outside Webb's Office door, his ear virtually to the wood. He could never have admitted that Webb had the power to surprise or entice him, yet he listened with the utmost attention. He had no idea what to make of this 'interview'. Webb had now arrived at the third party of workers.

" - whom he set to work in his third and last vineyard. At the end of the day he summoned his servants and instructed them to go and pay all the workers a day's wages. Now, when the first workers heard that the men in the second vineyard were to be paid the same as them, they were very angry and sought out the owner to protest. And when the second group of workers discovered they were to be paid the same as the third group, who had arrived after them, they likewise were very angry and they likewise went looking for the owner. They came across him sitting at his supper, drinking fine wine from his own vineyards. 'Why is it,' they cried, 'that you would pay the same wage to those who came later in the day?' The owner stopped eating and drinking and looked up at these ingrates. To the first group he said, 'I paid you fairly, did I not? You have a day's wages for a day's work?' The first group could not dispute this. 'Verily I say unto thee, be gone from my house. You came to my door in wretchedness to sell your labour, I put you to work and paid you what is due.' He then turned to the second party of workers. 'Have I not paid you a day's wages when you have but worked two thirds of a day?' The second group could not dispute this. 'Verily then I say unto thee, be gone from my house. You have been more than fairly paid.'"

For some reason the oration was brought to an end there. Neither Alec Webb nor John Fitzroy said anything more for several seconds. The third party of workers and the climax of the parable were set aside, forgotten. Gerry could imagine the tense, angry young carpenter sitting in that dusty kitchen chair before Webb's desk, smoking his cigarette and not knowing what to make of this, nor perceiving any guiding intelligence behind Webb's behaviour. The frustration of it. The humiliation. It was all

Gerry could do to stop himself from bursting in on them and saving Fitzroy from further torment.

"Now what, John," asked Alec Webb, "do you think is the point of that story?"

There was a pause, then John Fitzroy sighed.

"I have no fucking idea."

"There's no need to use language like that!" Webb snapped. "Do you think I'm impressed?"

"But I don't know what you're talking about, Mr Webb!" There was a note of genuine apology in the carpenter's voice. "I'm sorry but just let me have a look at that order book. Please. Someone's out there waiting for a loft conversion, and I'm sitting here listening to this. I don't get you, Mr Webb. You may mean well, but the biggest favour you could do me right now is to give me your order book and let me sort out a job. Why can't we just do that? Why not? Eh? Please. I'm asking. I'm begging, if you like."

"Any minute now you're going to lose your temper and storm out of that door again. But you won't have the courage to come back. Not a third time. Think about it, sonny."

"Oh fuck this." The carpenter's voice was lower, as if he were talking to himself now. "Fucking, fucking hell." He'd had enough. The interview was over.

Gerry quickly stepped back from the door and retreated inside the first bedroom.

Then the carpenter's voice was louder and clearer – to Webb. "Fuck this for a game of soldiers! I knew it. I knew I shouldn't have come back. My mum made me come back here and I knew it was a frigging waste of time."

The door opened and Fitzroy stood there in the doorway, looking back into the room. His neck was flushed with anger but his lean face remained deathly pale.

"You know what you are, Mr Webb? You're just a fucking wanker. That's all."

"My dear boy, that's a contradiction in terms."

"FUCK OFF! FUCK YOU!"

Fitzroy slammed the door and set off briskly down the broken stairs.

Since the door was one of the handleless, latchless doors on this floor it bounced back with the impact on the frame and came to rest against the wall again. Outside, Gerry stood a moment, his head down and his hands in his pockets. Then he stepped forward from the first bedroom of Mik and Kim's suite and into the Office doorway. Webb still sat behind his desk. His face was closed. The big lips were tightly sealed.

"How'd it go this time?" asked Gerry softly.

Sir Alec did not answer but held Gerry's stare with his small, bald eyes.

"Will you take him on this time?"

"You know," said Sir Alec, raising his chin, "you really are becoming rather a bothersome old man."

"Who are Kim and Mik, may I ask?"

"Kim and Mik," Sir Alec repeated. From somewhere he had taken out a pencil which he now tapped on the edge of his empty desk. "Kim and Mik are a delightful young couple who came in about a week ago, to the old Offices, looking for work, and, as it happened, were also in need of a home."

"So you brought them here."

"So I brought them here."

"Father Christmas himself."

Sir Alec smiled disarmingly. "That's me," he said.

"I am the landlord here. I am the only bona fide tenant in this building."

"Yes." Sir Alec nodded and stood up. "So you keep

saying. I wanted to speak to you about that." He came round from behind his desk, crossed the room and stepped past Gerry onto the landing. He stopped and turned when Gerry did not move. "Come on, then." Gerry followed him along the landing to the communal bathroom, which had served the three bedsits on this floor in better days. Once in the bathroom, which was quite spacious, Sir Alec stopped and lifted the lavatory seat. Gerry had expected something nauseous and unsightly but instead the bowl was clean and dry, just dusty about the sides. Where the water should have been there was a plug of coarse and stony concrete.

"What are you going to do about that?"

Gerry stared down into the bowl. He said nothing. Something in the coarseness of the concrete, in the dusty white china bowl, both fascinated and shocked him. It represented such a wilful act of state vandalism. He'd seen it before, of course, must have done, but had somehow forgotten about it.

Sir Alec continued. "The point is, Kim and Mik will have to share your ablutions, as it were."

Gerry frowned, still staring down into the bowl. A memory came to mind of some excreta around his lavatory bowl downstairs that he had cleaned away on his return from the police station. He had been at a loss to account for it. He knew his own habits well enough, and the lavatory was the one place where his standards had not yet fallen. It was the last bastion, the Maginot line. The thought that either of these two young lovers could come down to his floor, to his lavatory, without his permission, without even meeting him, without a by nor leave, and befoul his lavatory bowl and - *thinking no more about it!* - could leave him to clean up after him or her - "*Here, clean this up, gentleman Gerry!*" - Mik's shit or Kim's shit -

that thought was nothing less than maddening.

Gerry's eyes narrowed. He turned and nodded at Alec Webb.

"We'll see about that."

He turned and went back to his own floor.

Chapter Eight

Pleasures, Please

Music had always been one of Gerry's great loves. His knowledge not only of numerous concertos, symphonies and chamber pieces, but also of the biographies of the great composers, had set him apart in the staff room as a first authority on the subject. Several of the older staff had been fans of *My Music,* the weekly tv quiz with Frank Muir and Denis Norden, and of a lunchtime Gerry was regularly dug out from his club chair, where he sat recovering from the palpitations of the classroom, to come and resolve some petty dispute. And when a famous orchestra stopped off at Ipswich Corn Exchange, it was Gerry Delaporte who was asked for an opinion of its efforts, rather than the specialist music teacher - a pale young man with a droopy moustache who strummed folk songs on the guitar; a useless fellow who couldn't even play a hymn for assembly. (Neither could Gerry, as it happened, though it was widely assumed, with all his talk of keys and clefs, Britten and Beethoven, that he had a piano in his parlour that he tickled daily for Mrs Delaporte's delight.)

In Claremont Villas Gerry had learned to live without music and he'd made a virtue of necessity. Part of his motivation to go out and walk aimlessly about Notting Hill Gate, was just to catch the unexpected rush of sound from a shop doorway, or Portobello market stall, or even from some of the nearby flats. There was a first floor flat just a couple of streets away where some West Indians lived, and at the weekends their windows would be wide open, no matter what the weather, and there would always be one young man or another sitting half out of the window, sharing some of his Caribbean 'sounds' with the neighbourhood at large. Any music now had the power to move Gerry. Not for long perhaps, but if he disapproved or became bored, he could just walk on by. Oh, he knew well enough that reggae would drive him mad if it blasted within Claremont Villas itself, but to seek out a few moments of it a couple of streets away was a pleasant diversion on the way to the library. How spoilt he had been with his collections of classics at home in Ipswich. He had ruined his own ear. The tiniest imperfection had spoiled his precious pleasure. Things as they were now were curiously preferable. If some genie brought him a radio tomorrow, already tuned to Alun Rae on Radio 3, *Building My Music Library*, his life would not be enriched. He did not want any more to sit in perfect solitude listening to concerts he had never attended. He did not want any more advice on his record collection from the likes of Alun Rae – or to sit waiting, hoping, for the whole bloody programme, for Mr Rae to play one of his requests, which Rae had never played, not once, despite a thousand postcards from Ipswich, the Lake District and Provence.

No. All that kind of thing seemed masturbatory to him now. He wanted to get out and about, to join the broader currents of society, the strange orchestra of urban life all around him. And Gerry believed that this new sensitivity to a diversity of music, particularly modern music, with its shameless rhythms, might have something to do with his undampenable sensitivity to the soft moans, groans and gentle sighs of Kim and Mik in their sexual ecstasies.

He found these sounds harrowing but irresistible. They aroused feelings in him he had all but forgotten about. Not least, a rabid covetousness. Sexually it seemed Kim and Mik were a perfect coupling. Oh rare and lucky creatures to have found each other! This was why they had the two beds. They were so active, so tireless, one bed must have quickly become stale. Now Gerry understood what he had taken to be a curious match: the very young, brown eyed girl, with her fresh round face and her generous smile, taking up with the blunt-featured, though not ugly young man. This young man, this Mik, was a pleasure machine, a lover who could keep going just as long as she wanted, till Kim had come and come and come again and they were both played out. Gerry knew what they had found in each other, and so much older as he was, fifty-eight as he was, he envied them it so. To hear the music of their groans, their sighs, their cries, for up to half an hour or more, moved him more deeply than any concerto ever had. It cut right to the sad and rotten core of his life. If only he'd had just a few months of his own youth living with this physical intensity - just to possess the memory of having lived that way once, at the peak and satisfaction of mutual desire, to be able to remember that for himself, rather than feel this scourging jealousy for what he had never had, and now could never have. The truth was that even to hold another body in an affectionate embrace, and to be held by another similarly, through so many years of marriage, not even this had been part of his life. The irony, the tragic, stupid and pitiful irony of his married life! Oh, they had started out with something he supposed, a wanton giggling in the dark, but Anna had never relished the possibilities of sex, and the more he had tried to experiment, in his shy and anxious way, the more he had succeeded in repulsing her. He could remember from his own youth, even now, her response to his nudgings towards fellatio, his descents towards cunnilingus. "What do you think I am?" she'd asked, "A nymphomaniac?" That word, never heard between them before or since, coming from her, was charged with some unspeakable psychosis. That was it. That was the truth established for her. She wasn't frigid, it was just that he was perverse and only some aberrant desire would satisfy him. An attitude that represented the very best of English priggishness and ignorance. It was a turning point. He couldn't endure being embarrassed in that way.

There was too much time these days to reflect on such things.

Gerry had taken to leaving his rooms when he heard them start. He would come out onto the landing and stand there in the dark, in the cold, or sometimes in the early morning or the afternoon, and he would stand quite still, his head slightly bowed, and he would listen with all his concentration. He frowned if either of them said anything. He did not like that, he did not want that, he only wanted the raw voices without words. It was better if they used the nearer room, the one without the milk bottle wardrobe or bookcase or whatever it was. The sound was much clearer from this room. He thought that might have something to do with the handleless, latchless doors. They hadn't found a means of fastening them securely. This thought excited him intensely. It made him wince at himself with a guilty longing. When they were in the further room he sometimes moved onto the stairs. Not too far up, but it made such a difference to be a few steps towards their landing. Often they kept going for so long they outstayed him, and he would have to kneel down on the stairs, a squat, ageing figure, in dirty clothes, in the cold, a drip of mucus on the tip of his nose, bent quietly in the attitude of one at prayer.

One morning, when he knew they had both gone out, he re-visited their rooms.

He began with the further room, the one with the shelves. What a stable structure that was to stand the vibrations of such passion day in and day out! It had now been carefully laden with clothes. Her shelves were the upper ones, more accessible and of melamine or clean new wood. All the clothes there were neatly folded. He checked his desire to touch her various items of clothing. That knitted woollen jumper she wore most of the time, loose and rough and ready, paint-stained in places, which at the moment was lying clean here, its shape restored. Then he did touch it. Let his fingers run up and down the rows around her breasts. He moved on to her trousers. The blue corduroy jeans that were so close-fitting around the buttocks and crotch. Entering the house a few seconds behind them once, Gerry had stopped inside the door and watched them make their way playfully up the broken stairs, Mik with his hand deep in the back pocket of these blue corduroys. They negotiated the missing treads together, moving stiffly as one body from side to side, neither wanting to disturb Mik's caressing hand in that back pocket. Now, standing in their bedroom, Gerry shut his eyes and, just for a moment, put his hand on the crotch of her jeans and squeezed the cloth tight there. Then he pulled himself away and thrust his hands back in his Harris Tweed. He began a careful inspection of the rest of the room. He was not sure what to look for next, exactly, but he wanted more bits and pieces to add to his vision of their intimacy.

Next door the room was as it had been when he'd looked before, except that on the wall there was some childish calligraphy, a bit of Kim's handiwork, no doubt. He did not approve of it at all. Their names, ornately lettered, Mik's vertical, Kim's lateral, were joined at the K to form the single capital letter 'L' , and then of course after the 'L' followed 'ove', in smaller, plainer style. Gerry shook his head, making his disapproval known. Tsch tsch tsch . . . However, he reflected, walking idly about the bare room, pushed around by his covetous fixation, hands in pockets, an excess of sentiment was perhaps preferable to no sentiment at all.

Then his daily, or often twice, or thrice daily pleasure of listening to the young couple was interrupted. At first he thought nothing of it. He imagined, on returning from the library, or the police station, or from some walk or errand, and discovering that only one of them was in the house, that he had mistimed things. But then he noticed that they were seldom in the house together and when he met either of them on the stairs he or she had a dejected look. At night they were both there but, he deduced, they were now sleeping separately. They had fallen out. They had stopped 'making love'. Gerry felt nothing but impatience with them. He had quickly become accustomed to their new distraction and he resented having it taken away, particularly on account of some adolescent row, for goodness' sake. After a couple of days he was in a state of frustration quite as acute, he was sure, as they were. They were so stupid! Here they were, exerting their puny wills against the thrust of nature, which had brought them together as the one perfect coupling among thousands of disappointing and disconsolate affairs. If only he could say to them - *Get on with it! Please! Enjoy yourselves while you can!*

He heard Mik coming downstairs on the third day and rushed out to speak with him.

Who's that trip-trapping over my bridge?

"Mik," he said. Mik stopped and looked at him from underneath a rather unsightly and unfashionable fringe he had grown. His eyes were dull. Gerry thought for a moment that he might be on drugs or medication. Perhaps that's what was wrong. One of them had contracted some complaint and was under doctor's orders.

"Mik, look - " Gerry guided the young man's attention to his bathroom door. "Look here. I've taken off the lock. You and Kim can use my bathroom now. You don't have to go upstairs. That was mean of me. I'm sorry. I did it more to spite that idiot Webb than to get at you. I am sorry."

After Webb's remarks about the second floor lavatory, Gerry had fitted a hasp and padlock to his bathroom, forcing the new tenants to use the virtually open-air facilities on the third floor. Mik smiled uncertainly, and Gerry saw a charm in this half-sunny expression. He thought it showed Mik's gentle, humble spirit.

"Oh, right," Mik said. "Thanks." He couldn't look Gerry in the eye and his hands were buried in his donkey jacket pockets. He glanced down the stairway. "Thanks," he said again. He sniffed.

"But hadn't you better tell Kim? You must tell her. She might go upstairs again while you're out, and there's really no need. I know it's awful up there. Must be freezing. Best tell her now, don't you think?"

Mik made an odd, defeated sound, a sigh and a grunt at the same time, but he turned and went back up the stairs. Gerry listened from his landing. He heard Mik call Kim from outside the bedroom door, the further bedroom, the one with the shelves. Mik mumbled to her through the door.

"Bloke downstairs says he's opened up his toilet for us."

"Tell her I'm sorry!" Gerry called up the stairs, and was astonished at the fruitiness of his voice resounding on the cold and empty landings. "Tell her I'm sorry, Mik!"

"He says he's sorry."

There was no audible reply.

That afternoon Gerry stopped at an off-licence on his way back from the library. He bought a bottle of inexpensive Italian wine, one from a little too far North, and a corkscrew. This would mean virtually no food for the next two days until his Giro came through. The assistant in the off-licence wasn't going to wrap the wine for him, assuming it was destined for the nearest park bench, but Gerry, hardened to this kind of treatment now, insisted on it being wrapped. He wanted to present the bottle to Mik and Kim gift-wrapped in a sheath of white tissue paper.

On his return he did not give himself a chance to get nervous about the trick. He went straight up to the second floor. Mik was there, lying on his mattress in the first bedroom, his hands clasped behind his neck. There was a bulky paperback open on the floor, cover face up. *The Dice Man*, by Luke Rhinehart. *"Few books can change your life forever . . ."* shouted the quotation on the cover, *"But this one will! . . ."* MORE THAN ONE MILLION COPIES SOLD! Gerry knew the book. It had been passed around the staff room. A fatuous, ridiculous book. *The Dice Man*. And how much more fatuous and ridiculous did it look here, on the bare boards of Mik's bedroom.

Mik was staring up at the ceiling. He was clearly not relaxed, not comfortable with the thoughts his reading had inspired, uneasy about his next throw of the die and the options he had set himself that would change his life forever. There was something restrained in his attitude, as if he had to keep his hands behind his neck to stop them wandering elsewhere – down between his legs, no doubt. Numbers one to three meant he could have a wank, perhaps. Maybe right now he was revising those options from one to three, to one to four, and five, and six . . .

"Peace offering," Gerry said, holding up the bottle in its white tissue. "I really am so sorry about my meanness over the toilet."

Mik raised himself on his elbows. He frowned at the bottle of wine.

"Now, no fuss. Not a word. You owe me no thanks. Believe me when I say I am doing this for my own good. I must make some recompense. Enjoy it. Oh, and here's the corkscrew." He fetched the corkscrew with a flourish from the pocket of his Harris Tweed and tossed it gently onto the bed in front of Mik. He turned to go but then looked back: "It's for Kim too, of course. You have to share it! Share it to the last drop!"

"Thanks," said Mik. "Hey - " he gave Gerry his half-sunny smile again - "Cheers!"

It worked. And it was worth the deprivation of the few days without their music to relish the sounds that evening. The separation had made them more emotional. The lurchings from fierceness to tenderness were more extreme. Gerry stood out on his landing. They hadn't moved from Mik's room near the stairs. He worried that the combination of the emotion and the wine would make Mik reckless, he'd lose control and come too soon, but this did not happen. So determined must Mik have been to establish something lasting from this reunion he seemed to be exercising supreme self-discipline, and Kim's breathy pleasure was drunkenly unrestrained.

Gerry arrived at a new understanding of his enjoyment this evening. He realized that his moments of greatest excitement were those when he saw things from Mik's point of view alone, rather than envisaging them entwined in each other's arms, happily coupled. (That had its own pleasures, but of a lesser order). No, it was when he was on Mik's back, as it were, clinging on, watching Kim's pleasure from above, seeing her riven with excitement and desire, over which, vicariously, he held power - it was this power-crazed view that gave him greatest satisfaction, and it was this view which he now brought to sharpest focus. And, as he listened to them, words came to him - he stood there on the landing and the words came pell-mell in hoarse spasms under his breath. He heard Kim sigh tenderly to her lover, but under his breath Gerry snarled at Mik, whom he rode bare-backed, whom he whipped onward harder and harder, he snarled at him: *"Drive it in! Screw her down! Fuck her! Fuck her! Fuck her! Over and over and over!"*

He was so absorbed in this fantasy he did not notice Sir Alec Webb. He didn't hear or see him until he was actually there before him on the landing. They looked at one another and each of their expressions was tense and stern, but for different reasons entirely. Sir Alec misunderstood the fierceness in Gerry's eyes and the restraint in his stiff and crooked posture. He thought Gerry Delaporte - *Gentleman Gerry!* - was locked in a paroxysm of acute embarrassment. He shook his head wisely.

"This is what got them chucked out their last place, you know," Webb whispered, sharing this gossip with Gerry.

Webb's close breath, in the cold December air, was hot with some spicy eastern dish, and a distinctive trace of spirits – could it be gin? Gin and tonic? These smells of indulgence on his breath deepened his repugnance, at this of all moments.

What on earth are you doing here? – Gerry thought - *Standing about like some overgrown head boy!*

"I'm sorry, Gerry. I'll go and have a word."

But that's exactly right! You've just popped in to put the dorm lights out!

Gerry stepped forward and seized the sleeve of Webb's coat, "No!"

Webb looked into his eyes.

There was murder in Gerry's brown, watery eyes. "Leave them!"

Webb continued to stare into Gerry's face and Gerry returned the stare. In the shadowed light on the landing Webb's features were not clear, but Gerry could see well enough the bald eyes narrow and harden behind their fancy spectacles. Webb's eyes began to move, to explore Gerry's stubbly, dirty face, and his expression tightened into one of unutterable contempt. When at last he spoke his voice was clotted with feeling. "Why, you filthy maggot," he said. He stepped back, but Gerry, shrunken, crooked, still bent over his falling erection, clung to Webb's sleeve. Webb snatched his coat from Gerry's grip and started up the stairs. But he got no further than the third tread. Kim had begun to reach another climax, and then Mik joined her there, and the empty, derelict house reverberated with their ecstasy.

"Say nothing!"

Sir Alec glanced down at Gerry from a height far greater than the third tread, then continued up the stairs.

Not until he was back in his own bedroom did Gerry realize that when he had said to Webb, "Say nothing!", there had been but one thing on his mind. Webb himself would imagine Gerry was frightened that he would inform Kim and Mik that he had caught 'that filthy maggot Delaporte', that dirty old lecher, standing down there on the landing listening to them. But Webb would have been wrong, as always. That was not Gerry's concern at all. Such an anxiety was the very last thing on his mind. He did not care what Kim and Mik thought or felt about him, or what they did to him on account of what they thought or felt, for that matter. They could come down here to his rooms and beat him to pulp if they liked. They could kick his brains out. They would be most welcome. That did not matter in the slightest. His only concern was that if Webb did tell them then the sessions were at an end. It was this prospect he could not endure. His feelings were so intense on the subject he might have been in love.

But with whom? With whom?

There was a knock at the door.

"Who is it?" Gerry said.

They could kick his brains out. They would be most welcome.

"It's me. Alec."

"Go away."

"We need to talk a moment, Gerry."

"We do not."

"There's a couple of things, Gerry. Housekeeping . . . Might be to your advantage?"

Gerry stood from his kitchen chair and went to the door.

He opened it a few inches, just enough to speak through. Webb's face looked pale and elongated through the narrow aperture. All behind him was in total darkness now. No sounds from above. Mik and Kim were already in a drunken slumber, no doubt, lying in each other's arms. There was a dark exchange of draughts between bedroom and landing, affecting the temperature of neither. Webb's breath was foul with half-digested meat and Eastern spices and gin and tonic. That's what it was. G&T.

"What is it?"

"May I come in, Gerry? It's serious." Webb lowered his voice. "I'd rather not risk being overheard."

After a few second's hesitation, Gerry, anxious that there might really be some news about Kim and Mik, let Webb in and closed the door behind him. "What is it? You said housekeeping."

"Gerry," Sir Alec turned to face Gerry. "I want to say I'm sorry."

"Sorry? For what? What game is this?"

"Sorry for the way I spoke to you a few moments ago."

"Fuck off. I don't give a shit."

Sir Alec sighed. "Gerry, no one is taken in by this tough guy front."

Gerry watched his intruder move over to the window. From there, having consolidated his position in Gerry's bedroom, Sir Alec set his hands behind his back and turned once more to Gerry. He was like a Victorian father fulfilling some awkward parental duty.

"Housekeeping," Gerry reminded him.

Webb met his eyes and drew a deep breath. There was to be a pronouncement.

"Your wife ran out on you, Gerry."

The low sympathy in his voice gave the all clear now for a show of feeling from Gerry, for a dropping of the 'tough guy' guard, a breaking down, a helpless show of emotion.

Gerry had been so obsessed with the goings-on upstairs that he had hardly thought of his wife recently, and when he had, it had been to reflect on her performance as a sexual partner of some thirty years' standing. These reflections left him with feelings of great bitterness and recrimination. Her other more recent and material treachery paled into insignificance when compared to this. All the wasted years! Good God! But this was hardly a subject he cared to discuss with Alec Webb. He stared back at the tall and pious figure.

Webb lowered his head. His hands were still behind his back.

"That must have been a terrible blow, Gerry." He looked up, eager for Gerry to confide, hungry to share some dreadful moment of sentiment.

"You think so? Oh, I don't know," Gerry replied. He had suddenly seen another way of attacking Webb personally here, and all the sour and endless ruminations about his life, which he'd given such scope to over the last months, began to rise to the fore of his vindictive mind. "Maybe that's not been as bad as you seem to suppose, Mr Webb," he began. Gerry cocked his learned head and continued lightly: "My marriage was much like most marriages, I would imagine, and I can't see any necessity to lament its passing."

Webb looked grave.

"I know you'd love to think that I lament it, Mr Webb. That would suit you very well, I'm sure. But I do not. Not at all. I would rather be here right now than back where I was four months ago, with the other wretch I called my wife for thirty years. The break came rather late, to be sure, but better late than never." All this he delivered in very calm and reasonable tones, but slightly lilting tones.

"This is just the voice of your bitterness, Gerry."

"Oh, I don't deny that," Gerry retorted - still controlled, reasonable. "But what am I bitter about, Mr Webb?" Gerry took a hand from his pocket and wagged a finger at Webb. He felt excitement now in trying to shock this awful young man. "I'll tell you, shall I? I'll let you into the secret. I'm bitter about nothing less than the sheer - what shall we call it? - the sheer trumpery of my life. About what a dupe I have been to slavishly pretend, as everyone else pretended, that I could do a job which was utterly beyond me, or that I could live without a sex life, when I wanted to touch up every girl who set foot in my classroom . . ." He made a lewd, groping gesture with his right hand - feeling up a little girl's skirt, with wriggling fingers - a gross gesture he'd never made in his life before - "Put my hand beneath their little skirts . . . right up beneath their little skirts . . . Oh, it's dreadful, don't you think?" He stopped and put his hand back in his pocket. "And all my temptations, my afflictions, my bitterness, as you call it, add up to – to what? What would you say? To nothing more than the lot of the common man, I would think. The commonest of common men, don't you think?" He broke off and laughed at this self-evident conclusion, laughed at its newness, and at his own purblindness, at the understanding bubbling to the surface now quite spontaneously against his bidding. "One who lived out his life according to the rules, and covered up for himself as he went along, and took no bloody risks. That's it, you see! I took no bloody risks! Ever! Not until four months ago, anyway. What a woefully, horribly unexceptional little existence mine has been, eh?" He leant forward on his toes, hands in pockets, in the manner of the urbane schoolmaster he had never, ever been. "I'm glad only of one thing. That I can see my life for what it is - I can see it for the shabby piece of make-believe that it really is. And that's rather preferable to seeing it for what it isn't, which is what you'd like to do."

Webb bit his large underlip and stared back at Gerry. From this expression Gerry knew that he had failed again, he had not pierced the man at all. He had tried shouting at him, swearing at him, hectoring him and lecturing him, all to no avail. He wanted to speak again though before Webb came out with any further sanctimony. Glancing up at the ceiling he said: "It's nice to listen to them. It really is. Now there's a pleasure. A real pleasure. A treat, you know."

Webb looked grave again. Oh, that was so out of order, so without Christian decency.

"It's a new pleasure in my life. Very nice. Thanks for introducing me to Kim and Mik. There aren't many pleasures in Claremont Villas, let's face it! Perhaps you wouldn't enjoy it, though, Mr Webb. Perhaps you have a better sex life yourself. But somehow I think not. You are still young, yes, but you are ugly. You are unwanted. You are not in the market. Undesirable. Bad goods. Clobber. Junk. Just as I am old and undesirable and not in the market. Wrong generation. Out of date. Obsolete. Finished. Those two are enjoying what you have never enjoyed, nor I. Neither of us shall ever enjoy that. Can you believe it? You'd better, you know! What a waste, eh? Now there's a thought. At last we have something to share."

Webb took a deep breath.

"You never had any children, did you, Gerry?"

"No I didn't. I was a responsible parent. And please don't tell me you have children. That could only be a grotesque lie about grotesque progeny."

"No," Webb replied. "I have no children."

"Well then, let us not discuss a subject neither of us

knows anything about." Gerry took a step towards Webb - again he thought he saw a fissure in that bourgeois, Christian smugness. "Of course, that's not a premise you'd be likely to accept, is it, Mr Webb? Tell me, what on earth did you mean by sermonizing to that poor young man who came in here the other day? Sermonizing on - what was it? - ah yes! - " Gerry put a hand to his forehead and drew out the recollection with theatrical contempt – "The parable of the three vineyards. That was it. What on earth did you mean by telling poor Mr Fitzroy your parable of the three vineyards? I heard you, you see. I listened to every word outside your filthy little office!" Gerry twitched assertively, cocked his head, rocked forward on the balls of his feet. He chose his words with care. "How dare you practise your phony clericalism on the poor and deserving, denying them the opportunities they need to keep body and soul together? How dare you?" Gerry's eyes moistened with excitement again. He thought he saw a flicker of anxiety cross Webb's expression; he'd caught him on the hop, he'd hit a nerve at last. And suddenly Gerry felt full of vigour, as if all the sexual energy pent up in his ageing frame was finding release here in this invective against the young man in front of him. He took another step towards his quarry, and gone was his urbanity and sarcasm now. He pressed on at a brisk, aggressive tempo. "How dare you? Eh? I thought you said you wanted to help these people, give them some sort of work, and you wouldn't even give this fellow your bloody order book! Where is that order book, anyway? What's in it? What's in your order book? Nothing! Nothing at all! No one ever rings up your tuppenny Cooperative! No one gives a fuck about it! No one gives a shit! Two Strong Arms, indeed!" Gerry laughed viciously, a high, theatrical laugh. "And then if one poor deluded soul wanders in here at the end of his tether, having nowhere else to turn in his search for honest labour, what does he encounter? He encounters some Christian poseur, some public school nit, with nothing better to do because he was too stupid to enter the professional preserves of his class! And this Christian numpty then presumes to recount his parable of the three bloody vineyards! I ask you! I thought you were a joke, Webb, not worth the time of day - but you're not a joke. You're serious, and you've got to be told where to get off. It's not fair otherwise. That's it! It's simply not bloody fair! Shall I tell you what you need? Hmmn? You need to be beaten up in some back street! There's no other way. No amount of talk will do it. You need fists. You need revolution! Fists in the face! In those great rubber lips!" Gerry stepped closer still and shook his own feeble, fifty-eight year old fist at the impassive, impenetrable complacency of Webb's face. And he could do it. He could attack him. He was nearly there - "Fists in the face! A knee in the groin! You need to feel your elbows crack on the kerb as you go down! Then maybe you'd wake up! You'd see what we really think of you. I'm astonished that carpenter didn't take a swing at you - perhaps he's going to get a few friends together and they'll come and duff you up. Good! I hope so!"

Webb started to move towards the door, a manoeuvre which took him closer to his assailant, who stood his ground well enough, but who shook with emotion as Webb passed by.

Oh, what hell it was to be so full of feeling!

After opening the door Webb stopped.

"I shall not think a great deal about what you have said tonight, Gerry," he said quietly. "I'm sorry if that disappoints. But I shall think for a long, long time, a very long time, about the way in which you have spoken to me tonight. I shall think about your anger, and your hatred. You're not going to like this one little bit, but I shall pray for you. Pray very hard for you."

Gerry visibly sagged at that. The door closed. He heard Webb cross the landing and pick his way down the stairs in the dark.

Chapter Nine

£9000

It may have been nothing more than a coincidence, or it may have been that Sir Alec wanted to prove something to Gerry, but the day following Gerry's tirades things began to get organized for Two Strong Arms at Claremont Villas. From his landing Gerry looked on as Mik and Kim and some other ragged-arsed no-hopers staggered up the broken stairs with a filing cabinet, and, of all things, a rather elderly Chesterfield sofa. The diminutive Jake was there, struggling with the lower end of the Chesterfield on the broken stairs. Gerry did not lend them a hand, said nothing, only watched and scowled. Other oddments arrived. Potted plants, a scrap of carpet, one or two juvenile, frameless still lifes (Kim's art: she carried them up individually, and with great care), bits and pieces they used to personalize their Office, as if by doing so they made the idea of an office more genuine. Though he was curious to see the total effect - where would they put the Chesterfield? - Gerry kept sulkily to his own territory until the completion of the move, when some euphoria broke out upstairs and the atmosphere in the house became intolerable.

He would go to the police station and see what news they had there. It had been a week since his last visit. He had been told that an officer would call to see him if there were any developments, but he did not trust that. A personal visit was the thing. That was the way to keep them on their toes.

At the very moment that he stirred himself to leave, Alec Webb arrived to join the moving party, and as luck would have it they passed on the stairs. Webb was picking his way between the broken treads, head down, minding a rattan magazine-rack - something to be filled with copies of Punch, Gerry mused, for the entertainment of all the John Fitzroys waiting for their second or third or fifteenth interviews. But in the magazine rack this morning was lodged a magnum, no less, of chilled champagne, and a column of plastic cups. Condensation covered the green bottle. Once they had passed, awkwardly, eyes down, negotiating the few spaces of safe tread, Gerry heard Webb call up to his workers, jovial and patronizing, full of bonhomie and party spirit –

"Brought a little something to christen the move!"

Outside in the grey winter daylight Gerry found he had a hangover from the previous evening's excess. Perhaps he'd rather overstated his case against Alec Webb. The seed of his misgiving had been sewn by the sounds of the young people laughing together up there, friends joking together about the move, about where they were putting things, about where they should hang Kim's pictures, in an ironic, pleasant way; and yes, the friendly voice of Webb himself, who after all wasn't a great deal older than most of them, calling up to his comrades, his brothers and sisters in arms, affable, well-liked, respected. All of that camaraderie, which carried on oblivious to the sulky old troll downstairs, had quickened a jealousy in Gerry. He didn't want to hear Kim laughing when -

A thought stopped him dead.

He stood stock still on the pavement, in the December air, on which he could see his breath this morning. It was a moment of enlightenment, of epiphany even, right here on the corner of Lonsdale Road and Colville Road, under the sunken, dead belly of the sky. He stood there, rigidified, an obstruction to the door of the corner shop, the newsagents-cum-minimarket. A young woman with a pushchair rushed up behind him. He did not move. Could not move. She hesitated until her infant started to bawl, then she muttered crossly at Gerry and shoved her way round him into the shop.

Good grief.

Was it true?

Was that it, then? Was he now alone in the world, for ever and ever, amen?

Could he look forward to absolute solitude for the rest of his days? Surely somewhere out here was another creature with whom he could form a last minute coupling before the music stopped? Surely there was someone out there who -

To think one could live to the age of fifty-eight, nearly fifty-nine years, meeting God only knew how many scores of people, and yet, in all that time, all these years, strike up so few lasting friendships with persons of either sex . . . Well, that wasn't really so surprising, if you really thought about it, because despite all the evidence to the contrary, all the sprawling conurbations, people didn't really want to live together at all, if you gave it a moment's thought. Man as a social animal was a lot of nonsense. He had social needs, right enough, but he wasn't social. On the contrary, he was antisocial, he was a bloody little misanthropist, when you got right down to it. Given half a chance he bought privacy and isolation from his kind. He put up walls and fences. As soon as he had some money he built a private swimming pool, not a pool for everyone to swim in. People simply needed the illusion of belonging to a wider community. Gerry considered for a moment that he had dispensed with all such illusions, that he was the only one living in his true and natural state, belonging nowhere, to no one, making up his own values, living for the moment, existential man - that awful phrase! - but it was not a comforting or pleasant reflection. It was difficult to say with any dignity: I belong nowhere, and to no one.

But was it true? That there would be no further physical, and yes, sexual, companionship in his life? Was that it? Finished? That part was over, forever?

The answer was, apparently: Yes, indeed, old chap.

With heavy step he walked on. He passed the newsagents-cum-minimarket.

There was a need though, wasn't there, a simple human need, something instinctual, animal even, to hold another body, and to be held by another body. For so many years Anna had never gratified that need for him (nor he for her, for goodness' sake). Though for her, perhaps, there had been no need for him to gratify it, because for her, in recent times - for years, perhaps – maybe thirty bloody years! – there had been someone else to gratify it. Webb's *compagnon*! True or untrue, how ridiculous. For him, the simple fact they had shared the same roof had meant he could at least pretend, or assume, the satisfaction of such a need was at hand, and therefore not worry about it - not quite so much. What a way to carry on, eh?

And carry on, and carry on. He dragged his steps to Ladbroke Grove Police Station.

Two men – two other, lone men - one young and black, one old and white, were already waiting at the counter to see the Desk Sergeant, who was not at his desk, of course. Gerry took a seat and waited his turn too. He was relieved that he had to wait. He felt quite unfit for any kind of human interaction just at the moment. The Desk Sergeant, delayed by some humorous conversation in an office doorway, at last returned to duty with a fresh cup of tea and a plate of biscuits.

Gerry eavesdropped on the strange and trivial matters of illegality brought to the attention of the duty officer this morning. It transpired that the young man, a tall and wiry fellow, Mr Osmah, was in the throes of starting up his own car-valeting business, and he had been very badly cheated. He had not been paid a penny for his labours, not by any of the local garages on whose forecourts he'd waxed and shined, seven days a week, for the last month or so. And he was seriously out of pocket for all his wax, his buckets, his chamois. It took just a couple of curt questions, between dunking and eating a triangle of Garibaldi, for the Desk Sergeant to establish beyond all reasonable doubt that Mr Osmah never would be paid, not a penny, neither for his labour nor his materials. That was that. Case dismissed. Mr Osmah turned and retreated, a wounded, riven look in his dark eyes.

The old white man was a night security guard. Every evening he travelled up to Tottenham, where he guarded an abrasives factory from 9 p.m. to 6 a.m. His problem was that he could get no sleep during the day on account of a neighbour's Alsatian dog, which was cooped up in the flat above while its owner was out at work. It barked all day, every day. It was intolerable. It was a public nuisance. That phrase 'public nuisance' was repeated a few times, bandied about. The Desk Sergeant wanted the old man to let go of the phrase, but he wouldn't. Having fetched out his own tiny wafer of legal jargon the old man held on to it, despite all the pushing and pulling of the Desk Sergeant. In the end he was grudgingly lent a Biro and directed down the counter for some punitive form filling.

Gerry rose and approached. The Desk Sergeant now stood very upright, in an obstructive, impatient mood. No one else would pass this morning.

But as soon as Gerry introduced himself a curious thing happened: the Desk Sergeant held up his hand, turned, and without a word withdrew to the offices to consult with his colleagues. He returned with Detective Sergeant Tenmere in person, and Gerry was invited by that officer to come behind the counter and join him in one of the interview rooms. Tenmere had with him a bulky clipboard of notes. By the way in which he was treated now, with a new courtesy, a new gravity of purpose, Gerry deduced that success came rarely to these people in their work, and that his 'case', such as it was, had turned out to be one of the more promising the C.I.D. had taken on.

Once seated in the interview room with the door closed behind them, there was a pause. They sat opposite one another, either side of a smart Formica table with dark hardwood edging. The silence lengthened. D.S. Tenmere, C.I.D., was giving time for some dramatic tension to develop. His face was very grey, as if he'd spent all his life under the strip lights of the interview room, and there was a heavy five o'clock shadow around his blunt and protuberant jaw. To Gerry, who did not trust any of the policemen he had met to date at Ladbroke Grove, Tenmere's face brought to mind the comic strip image of a burglar: the masked man on the run with a bag of swag. His shifty eyes were sunk beneath an overhang of forehead and unruly black brows. They seemed to hide away under there from the strip light of the interview room.

"I think we've got her," he said at last, with the customary grim satisfaction. He nodded to Gerry, as if they shared a personal understanding, which they did not. "We've found her."

"My wife?" Gerry asked. "That's good news. Very good news. Where is she?"

"She's holed up in Wales."

"Wales?"

Wales? How on earth had they come to that conclusion? Particularly given the passivity of their procedures.

"Wales?"

Tenmere nodded, certain of his facts. "North Wales. By the sea." He consulted the papers on his clipboard. "Pwllheli. Little tourist place. Beautiful spot."

Gerry frowned. This seemed unlikely in the extreme. Too northern. Too rural. Too remote. Anna had never much shared his taste for the idyllic. He had imagined that she'd taken herself off to another town or city, where she could be immersed, hidden, and where there was some prospect, at least, of a new social scene of some description. He couldn't imagine what might have tempted her about a place like Pwllheli. Still, she was by the sea and that fitted; that at least was what he had expected. And given that she had second-guessed him for so long, he could hardly argue the point.

"The identikit matches *exactly*."

The officer laid such stress and conviction on his last word it was plain he was talking here about an infallible method of detection. Having seen a few of the earlier portraits of his wife, some of which were simply ridiculous, making Anna look like a harridan, a termagant, a witch, Gerry was inclined to think otherwise.

"Do you have anything else?" he asked. "I mean, how did you come to this conclusion?"

"There's a lot of circumstantial." Again the knowing nod. "Let me take you through it." He bent up the spring of the clipboard and reset his notes squarely beneath it. But he didn't need his notes. He knew it all by heart. He inhaled noisily through flared nostrils and let the spring snap back on the clipboard. He looked up at Gerry, and began.

"Suspect let a small cottage near Pwllheli two days after you left Ipswich, and then moved in there one week from that date, on August 14th." Tenmere paused, allowing Gerry time to absorb these primary facts. "As I say, nine days after your departure on August 5th. The house clearance people cleaned out Rosebery Road on August 20th. Quick work. She executed sale of house and contents as fast as she could after your departure, then did a runner. She took a rock-bottom price for the house, and I mean rock-bottom. Would you believe nine thousand pounds?"

Gerry stared back at the policeman. At the granite features of Detective Sergeant Tenmere.

But he must be strong here. He must be Roman.

Oh dear, though, for goodness' sake, for Jesus Christ's sake, it was such a blow. He really hadn't thought, hadn't imagined this. He felt quite breathless. Nine thousand pounds. £9,000. The number triggered some calculation in his brain, some unstoppable quantification, crystallization. Yes, he could feel it, the flat, flawless surfaces of a crystal growing, pushing, cutting, squashing, deep within the cerebellum. He felt unbalanced. Then, in a rush, with a skull-cleaving pain, a migraine broke out across his forehead. It made him shut his eyes it was so explosive, so maddening and vicious.

Nine thousand pounds.

£9,000.

It was suicidal!

But of course, she had never actually *earned* the money to pay the mortgage, never actually sold her life, sold her soul, to pay the mortgage, so why should she care?

How could she *know*?

"She only went back to collect the proceeds of the clearance, and finalize the sale of the property with dear old Maidment and Co.," Tenmere continued. "Incidentally, you might just have a case against them. A most negligent bunch of scriveners, in our view."

Gerry frowned, but not to query what the officer had said, which in some important aspects tied in with his own fears and suspicions. No, he frowned because he was pained to hear that his wife, Anna, had actually done these things. That she had been to Maidment's offices. That she had made an appointment for the house clearance people to come round – not too early, at eleven-thirty, perhaps, after elevenses. That she had, in Tenmere's phrase, 'done a runner'. It was difficult to imagine this woman of fifty-nine doing a runner, but the thought that she had done so, and the lengths she had apparently gone to, the recklessness of her behaviour and yet her thoroughness, her organization, all of this spoke of a determination on her part to be rid of her husband once and for all. And though all this had been obvious enough to Gerry for the best part of a month now, it was only here, today, in the clean bright interview room, at the Formica table with the hardwood edging, when his fears and suspicions were proudly given grounds and substance by the grey faced Detective Sergeant Tenmere, it was only here and now that it all became real and true. That it all crystallized.

"My car?"

"Cash sale."

Tenmere uncovered a note on the clipboard.

Here we go, said Gerry to himself. Brace yourself.

"Fiveways Autos, Ring Road, Ipswich."

Gerry knew the place. Shabby. Disreputable. *Same-Day Clutch Repairs. Brake linings. Exhaust Bays . . .*

"Rock-bottom price again, I'm afraid. Really rock-bottom. A bit sad, this one. Eight-fifty for an 'L' reg Escort. Wish I'd known! My daughter's just passed her test!" Tenmere chuckled a moment, distracted.

Congratulations, Gerry nearly said.

"Such is life. Coincidentally, that sale only went through after all the other business in Ipswich was completed. It all links up, you see."

It all links up, thought Gerry. He's right. It all links up. There was indeed a lot of circumstantial.

"The Spanish people?"

"Chilean, actually. The Peiriahs." The Detective Sergeant took pride in pronouncing the name correctly. He had done his homework down to the very last detail. "The Peiriahs didn't move in until September 12th. Our sources in Pwllheli confirm that there was some toing and froing when your wife first arrived at the cottage. She was absent for the whole day, or for two days on a few occasions. She always returned at night. Very late. Wee small hours. The landlady knows that because she lives just above the place and keeps a very close eye on it. Bit of a busybody, actually. Nosey parker. But that's in our favour – she gave us the tip-off in the first place. The comings and goings fit with the fact we could find no trace of your wife in any of the hotels around Ipswich. We rang round."

Gerry was dubious on this point. "It's a long way. And my wife is not a young woman."

The officer nodded.

"She probably broke the journey. Overnight stop somewhere. Motel. Little Chef. B and B. Maybe slept in the car. She's a tough cooky, and shrewd with it. Always thinking well ahead. A real hard-nosed little operator."

Again Gerry frowned. He did not like to hear his wife described in this police vernacular, but he didn't know quite how to stop it. The officer assumed he wouldn't mind, that he might share, and even enjoy, this combative attitude towards his wife, but Gerry felt uneasy. Clearly from their investigations and from their identikit pictures the police had invented their own version of Anna Delaporte, some scheming, ruthless bitch, worthy of their own image of themselves. But it wasn't quite as simple as that. Not to Gerry. Or wasn't it? Wasn't it, in fact, just as simple as that? A scheming, ruthless, treacherous bitch.

"The landlady says it was your car but she never actually took the number - a great shame, really - and then by the time we started our enquiries it hadn't been around for months. Frankly she doesn't know much about cars. But she's sure about the colour. Identical colour. She's certain of that. Nevada Beige?"

Gerry nodded, though the name, the colour, meant nothing to him at all right now.

Nevada Beige.

Beige. Like his creaseless trousers. Beige. Worthless. Grubby. Baggy. Beige.

The Detective Sergeant narrowed his eyes. "Now suspect just uses taxis, mini-cabs – hardly ever the same one. This one's really given us the run-around. A proper tease."

"Now wait a minute - " Gerry raised his hand - "there's no need for language like that." But then he winced at himself, realizing he had borrowed a turn of phrase from

Alec Webb. This interview was all getting too much – D.S. Tenmere, the Formica table, the horrible light, his horrible wife, Nevada Beige, the rough talk - all quite insupportable. He must draw it to a close somehow. He sighed and dry-washed his face. "Just let me think about what you've said a moment, Sergeant. Those details . . ."

The Detective Sergeant nodded patiently.

Gerry set his leathered elbows on the Formica, covered his eyes with his hands, and pondered upon what he had been told.

This was quite a case they had built up. It was strange to imagine that while he did whatever he did with his days - visiting the library during the afternoon, kneeling on the landing to listen to Kim and Mik, masturbating in his bedroom - that while he went about the business of his days, the nation's police force, at his behest and the tax-payers' expense, rang round hotels, house removals firms and secondhand car-dealers in and around Ipswich, chasing down his runaway wife. Fiveways Autos. Same-Day Clutch Repairs. Exhaust Bays . . . Well, he wasn't going to complain, and though he had some nagging doubts he felt it would be churlish to press them at this stage. By all accounts the time of reckoning was nigh. He felt a rush of adrenalin at that thought. He had been distracted from this possibility of late, but now that it had been brought so forcibly to mind again all his other preoccupations paled into insignificance. The prospect of regaining his assets, though somewhat diminished, transformed his outlook on life. He could be free of Notting Hill within days, within a week at the most. The question remained of course - *What had Anna done with his money?* Nine thousand pounds. Eight hundred and fifty pounds. And he regarded it as *his* money now. She could live out the rest of her days in some bedsit somewhere.

Yes. Let her taste some penury. He'd give her the address in Notting Hill. He'd write it down for her. Here you are, dear. See how you make out there with Alec Webb, and Kim and Mik, Jake and Two Strong Arms! Hah! He could not have cared less. He was off. He was going abroad. To France. To Provence. He would buy himself a little car, that little open-top car – at last! - and tour those hot, straight roads lined with poplars. Money, of course, was the most important thing in life. Money was freedom of movement, freedom of choice, not to mention the bread in the mouth, the very sustenance of health and morale, the mortar that bonded body to soul. All, everything, was utterly dependent upon it. Why had he never properly understood that? What a silly distraction his education had been, when you got down to brass tacks. So, he would have some money once more, and he wouldn't have to buy for two any longer. Bravo! What a saving. What had she been doing with his pension, he wondered. Not a great deal, by the sound of it. Apart from the understandably reckless sales early on it would seem she had been husbanding his finances quite admirably - for her own sake, of course, but now he would swoop down to regain all.

Gerry lowered his hands and knitted them on the table in front of him.

"I'd like to thank you for your work on this case, Detective Sergeant Tenmere," he said with some dignity. "If this suspect does indeed turn out to be my wife, you will have saved me from at best an old age of destitution, and at worst an early grave. Perhaps that should be the other way around, in fact. I thank you. I do. I thank you. Please pass on my thanks and congratulations to your colleagues."

A small and awkward smile opened in Tenmere's five

o'clock shadow. "All part of the service," was all he could muster in response to Gerry's gentlemanly courtesy.

"Will you now bring the suspect to London?"

Tenmere shook his head emphatically. "No, no. It can't be done like that. Protocol. You must go up there and an interview will be arranged in the local nick. We can't go dragging her all the way down here before identification. Could be very messy."

"I see." Gerry was puzzled. This could be an unfortunate hitch. "Will I be taken up there, then?"

Tenmere chuckled at the very idea. "No, no . . . I'm afraid not. You'll have to make your own way. And the quicker the better, obviously. I'll give you all the details. If the identification is positive, which is really a foregone conclusion as far as we're concerned, *then* the two of you will come back here for the charges. It might be an idea to give me the name of a solicitor, by the way. Presumably not dear old Maidment and Co.!" Tenmere chuckled again.

Gerry didn't respond. He was pressed by more immediate concerns.

"But how am I to get up there, then? You know I have no money. Is there some police fund I can borrow from? The Criminal Injuries Board, or something?"

"No, no . . . I'm afraid not."

"Well, what am I to do?" Gerry was irritated by Tenmere's unimaginative responses. "Hitchhike? To North Wales?"

But then, almost as if it were an afterthought, the Detective Sergeant solved the problem.

"The social security will sort out an emergency payment for you," he informed Gerry. "It's standard procedure in a case of this kind, where one party is without adequate means. It's not a problem."

Gerry was relieved. "Yes. That's me," he said, "most

certainly. Without adequate means."

"I'll see to it. It's no trouble." Tenmere stood up and left. In a few moments he returned with some headed stationery on which were typed some five or six lines above a brief form. "This will suffice. It's a standard letter." Tenmere leant down to complete and sign the document. "D.S. Aldwich will look after you up there."

"A Detective Sergeant?"

Tenmere looked up from the form. "Yes. A Detective Sergeant."

"But won't an Inspector - "

"No no. Not at this stage. Aldwich is a fine officer. He'll look after you. We started out together, actually. In Wiltshire."

Tenmere signed the letter and presented it to Gerry. "Aldy will look after you all right." Gerry quickly read the letter, the form – Aldwich's name was there on the form - folded the document and put it safely away inside his Harris Tweed.

"I'm very much obliged to you, Detective Sergeant Tenmere," he said, standing and holding out his hand across the clean Formica table.

Gerry was in a much lighter mood on returning to Claremont Villas than he had been on setting out. He was feeling so chipper, so chirpy, that he tried to catch up with Alec Webb, who had only just left the house. The festivities of Two Strong Arms must have been quite protracted. Webb was some fifty yards ahead, walking down Lonsdale Road towards Colville Road and Colville

Mews. He'd set up a brisk pace, as if in a hurry to get out of the weather. His hands were tucked deep into his coat pockets and his collar was turned up against the cold.

So high was Gerry's confidence he fully intended to try and touch Webb for a loan, so that he might assist with police inquiries this very evening, or first thing tomorrow at the latest. Suffer no delay! And with this loan avoid all the maddening aggravation with the social security officers, and their unpredictable and fantastical procedures. Act independently. Take the initiative. Now! He was prepared to make his peace with Webb, of course, and offer all manner of abject apology and phoney contrition, so long as it resulted in his taking from Webb's wallet the cost of the rail fare. He had no doubt it could be done easily enough. Underneath all Webb's pretensions and Christian sentiment the man was a soft-hearted fool, anyone could see that - a magnum of champagne, no less! For the workers! Gerry had no doubt he could sting him for a 'pony' at least.

He crossed to Webb's side of the road and redoubled his pace.

But just as he was about to close on his quarry a taxi pulled out of Colville Mews and Webb instantly flagged it down. Gerry heard Webb give his destination as he shut the door behind him. The door slam clipped off the last syllable but Gerry was pretty sure he'd got it right.

Observatory Gardens.

Though he knew little about London, his idle wanderings had taken him into the richer neighbourhoods hereabouts many times. Gerry was fond of walking around those parts, the nests of mews and lanes between Holland Park and Kensington Gardens. He liked staring up at the Regency town houses in their fresh magnolia, with their scrubbed steps and polished knockers. Unless he was mistaken, Observatory Gardens was just such an address. It went with names like Gordon Place and Gloucester Walk and Vicarage Gardens. Inspired by his visit to the police station this afternoon Gerry felt an impulse now to do some detective work of his own. He was going to visit Observatory Gardens. He would go this very evening. It couldn't be a long street, and he knew well how the residents of that neighbourhood liked to leave their polished windows uncurtained late into the evening, turning their living rooms into display cabinets.

What an interesting adventure lay before him tonight.

Chapter Ten

Observatory Gdns.

On his way out that evening Gerry stalled a moment on the landing: Kim and Mik had just started their ascent towards another climax. He only stopped long enough to ask why this suddenly meant so little to him, then put his keys in his pocket and pressed on. He didn't like the idea that his moods were volatile and flimsy things, windblown by hormonal highs and lows. It smacked of infirmity again. But there had been enough introspection recently. Quite enough. Just get on with it, he told himself. Just do what you were going to do, and see if you can't enjoy yourself for once.

It was no more than a twenty minute walk to Observatory Gardens. His daytime strolls had led him to Kensington Gardens often enough, and to get to this evening's destination he simply took a left off Kensington

Church Street, down Gloucester Walk, or Campden Grove. It all looked very straightforward on the map, but he had his Nicholson's Streetfinder wedged into his jacket pocket in case of any unforeseen complications.

Shortly before six o'clock, unfatigued and still in good spirits, he arrived at the junction of Campden Grove and Hornton Street. Observatory Gdns. lay directly opposite. It was not a street he recognised in any way and he couldn't recall ever having strayed down it before. His visits to this area had been restricted to the Kensington Palace side of things. He looked suspiciously up and down Hornton Street, with its imperturbable residences. Why was it always so much quieter where rich people lived? As if those behind the stately facades were listening, alert to any intrusion upon their peace and quiet, ready to fold away their newspapers or close their magazines and call out - *Who goes there*? With a wince Gerry dismissed such nonsense - really, the attitudes penury bred in one's soul. One had to be forever on one's guard against such stuff.

A Jaguar pulled away from the nearside kerb. He waited for it to pass then struck out across the road.

Tall and distinctive, the houses of Observatory Gdns. were set in a short crescent and were well illuminated, well exhibited even, by a row of converted nineteenth century gas lamps. Conservation meant something to the people here. All the lamps glistened with gloss green paint. And they shed such light! Burglars beware! Even the uppermost floors of the houses were visible, right up to the circular attic windows, bedded in feathered slate. These magnificent houses were to his right. To his left was a row of expensive cars and then a generous space, with some trees, bench seats, more lamps, more expensive cars, before the Campden Hill Court apartments. It was all rather nice. Very pleasant indeed. Gerry stopped at a tourist plaque which gave him more cultural and historical background to Observatory Gdns. Sir James South, the astronomer, had built, on this site, in 1831, what was then the largest telescope in the world. After his death the site was sold to Thomas Cawley, who built the houses now standing in the 1880s. Fascinating. Gerry hung around by the plaque, glancing about, his hands behind his back, as if he were on the fringe of a party of sightseers here, being addressed by a tour guide. There were twelve houses altogether in the crescent, each with its own hefty flight of eight steps to the front door, each front door with its own stained glass panels and soft hallway lights beyond.

Gerry stepped back from the houses towards the cars, the Jaguars and BMWs and Mercedes, all parked to attention, bristling with badges and permits and privileges. He edged between a brace of Porsches to the rear of the car parking space, where a dwarf wall separated this parking zone from that belonging to the Campden Hill Court apartments. Several trees interrupted the dwarf wall at regular intervals. Everything, to the last detail, was thoughtfully and aesthetically arranged.

But now that he was here in Observatory Gdns., his cause seemed spurious, absurd. The surrounding wealth in some way belittled his petty scheming and made him feel foolish. His shoulders sagged, his hands unclasped behind his back and fell lifelessly at his sides. He was no longer on the fringes of a tour guide's group. Here in Observatory Gdns. he was, he was - what? He was trivial. He was irrelevant. It would be better just to go away, forget all about it. But then he remembered Webb himself getting into that cab at Colville Mews, and he imagined that cab drawing up at the kerb opposite, and in his mind's eye he saw Webb leaning forward from the back seat and paying the cabbie and then opening the door and stepping forth -

and this was all too much for him. He would have a quick look around. He was here now and he would see the thing through, silly though it was. If by any chance he happened upon the Webb residence, he would swiftly pass by and take stock from a safe distance, and then reconsider his position. He might decide to knock brazenly at the door and bid good evening; he might throw a brick through the window; he might try his hand at a little arson; or he might set off back to Notting Hill to fetch Kim and Mick, find Jake, raise a mob, start the revolution. There was no point in speculating about what he would do. In all likelihood he would discover nothing and return to Claremont none the wiser.

He left the dwarf wall and came back between the Porsches to the crescent itself and began his inspection. He started at a gentle pace. He had an unobstructed view through the ground floor windows, raised from street level by four feet or so.

No sooner had he set out on his half-hearted plan than he nearly ruined everything. He had passed just two houses when there, in number 3 Observatory Gdns., was his man, his quarry. There was Alec Webb.

It was he. It was him.

There could be no mistake. There was Alec Webb, at home. At least, he certainly looked as if he were at home. Perfectly at home.

Gerry hastily retreated between the cars and mounted the dwarf wall. This offered him an angled view of No. 3. The curtains of the living room, just as he had imagined, were not drawn, and the view within was boastfully uncluttered. Webb himself was sitting in solitude on a long, pale green sofa. He wore a red cashmere sweater, with a crew neck that secured the collar of his shirt in his preferred style. He looked exceedingly comfortable. He was reading something. A glossy magazine. And apparently he had just eaten. Now and then he worked at a food particle stuck between his incisors with his fingernail. There could be no doubt about it. He was at home. This was the Alec Webb residence, if you please.

Gerry stood dead still, as if unable quite to absorb what his eyes beheld. He was so conspicuous, standing there on the dwarf wall, that he might as well have had his nose pressed up against the plate glass of Webb's living room window.

But what a discovery this was.

Someone entered the room, turned and gently closed the door, then approached Webb's sofa. For a few seconds, throwing caution to the winds, Gerry stayed where we was, staring at this other person, transfixed, then he got down from the wall, squeezed back between the cars and retraced his steps quickly to the start of the crescent, his head down, his mind in tumult.

Though he had only seen the person entering the room for a few seconds, the impression she had made was quite indelible in every way. She was a very beautiful young woman, small in stature, dark in complexion, of Asian extraction. Her long black hair was fastened with a gold clasp at the back - Gerry particularly remembered that sudden glint of gold as she turned to close the door. She had been bearing a bronze tray with a drink in a tumbler, cut glass no doubt. Waterford crystal, no doubt. She wore a soft, pale blue jumper and a fine red pleated skirt which ended just above the knee. On her feet . . . Gerry had not seen her feet, but for some reason the idea popped into his mind that she wore nothing on her feet, that her feet were bare, naked. This speculative detail, this mere suspicion, was no sooner born than it became a certainty more powerful than any other detail he had actually seen. It suggested an ease, a disregard, which signified to Gerry a physical intimacy, a sexual intimacy, with the only other person in the room. With Alec Webb. This must not be. It could not be. No shoes, no tights of any kind, the leg naked from the toe to the ankle, to the calf, to the knee, to the skirt, and beneath the skirt, to the thigh. And the lovely young woman had held before her that tray of ancient bronze, with the glass, filled with a bubbling drink intended for none other than Alec Webb, Old Gordonstounian, erstwhile schoolfellow of royalty and nobility, Lord of Claremont Villas, Notting Hill Gate, W11.

Gerry's breath was short. What a discovery this was! What violent feelings it aroused within him. This was no would-be priest, this Alec Webb, this was an Archbishop manqué! And to imagine that he solemnly left this residence each day to go and mix with Mik and Kim, to interview John Fitzroy - *Do you know, John, what a parable is? Joseph was a carpenter, you know. Did you know that?* - and perhaps, if he had the spiritual strength after all of that, he might put in some overtime counselling an elderly, derelict schoolmaster, an outcast, a very bitter man who had been deserted by his wife, who had lost everything he had, and had fallen by the wayside; a man as yet too traumatized to accept there was such a thing in the world as a good Samaritan. This was a particularly difficult case for the pastor, demanding great patience and tolerance and finesse. Then at eventide, the day's labours at a close, the pastor hailed a taxi and returned to Observatory Gdns., those built by Thomas Cawley in the 1880s, the very same. Supper was served and eaten, and then he had some postprandial tipple, which he needed in order to wind down from the strains of the day, the spiritual life, and his drink was served on a brass tray by this lovely girl, and the tray, no doubt, had been engraved and beaten by some legless beggar in Calcutta.

Well, Gerry considered, there would be no mistake this time. There would be no living this down for Alec Webb. This time the Christian cockroach would be utterly crushed. Gerry turned around. He assessed the various vantage points. A closer, longer inspection was required. Immediately.

Fifteen feet or so from where he had been standing on the dwarf wall was a stripling tree, a poplar or something, not a very substantial tree but one that would offer enough cover from the point of view of Webb's living room. Cautiously Gerry started back up the crescent. He edged alongside the first parked car, mounted the wall, and proceeded quickly as he could, one foot in front of the other on the narrow wall, to the tree. He glanced about and, stooping slightly, took up position, snug to the slender tree. This tree, as yet a straggling, adolescent bit of nature, actually turned out to be a bit of a nuisance, because though it didn't have many lower branches, those it did have were at eye level, so that Gerry had to stretch up in order to gain a good view of the living room interior.

The young woman - surely she was no more than a girl? - had left the tray and drink on a rosewood table to the side of the sofa. She was still in the room. She was standing at a long desk or table set against the wall behind the sofa, apparently sorting some papers. Some secretarial work for the diocese, no doubt; for the diocesan newsletter, perhaps, which was to be distributed by Jake or Mik or some other some ragged-arsed no-hoper from Two Strong Arms at the end of the month. Yes. Oh yes. Gerry saw it all now. Understood it all. Webb reached for his drink, sipped it and replaced it. Narrowing his eyes, Gerry spotted a sliver of yellow in the glass, which would identify the drink as gin and tonic. Webb leant back a moment so that his neck rested on the top of the sofa, and said something up to the ceiling. Directly he spoke, the young woman squared her papers and stopped what she was doing. She turned and approached the back of the sofa. Webb was idly flicking through his magazine again. She rested her hands on his shoulders and began gently to massage Webb, while he carried on flicking through the pages, stopping at this picture or that picture, occasionally sipping his drink. Then he raised a hand and she took it. This was a signal of some kind. She stopped the massage and moved round the arm of the sofa, where she stood next to the side table. Webb's right hand came round her now and began to stroke her behind the knees.

Gerry shut his eyes tight. His breathing had quickened. At fifty-eight, very nearly fifty-nine years of age, he seemed to be more stirred by erotic feeling than he ever had been in his youth. Everywhere he went he was surrounded by sexual activity these days. Yet here, in this scene, those feelings were tempered by confusion with other feelings just as powerful and instinctive. He hated this Alec Webb, and with a quite irrational ferocity. He did not think he had ever disliked anyone, even any of his tormentors at school, quite as much as this. Even for his wife, where there was surely provocation enough, he did not feel anything approaching the loathing he felt for this man. For Gerry Delaporte, Webb had taken on a burden of blame and shame that even the man himself, for all his pastoral posturing, would have found quite astonishing. For Gerry, Webb embodied the quintessence of his class, that impenetrable smugness, that dandified English uselessness, which survived the ages no matter what, that lived on regardless, all powerful, insulated by irreducible wealth and privilege. Gerry felt a rabid resentment towards

Webb that gnawed his innards, and nothing could content his soul till it was assuaged.

He opened his eyes now to see that which he dreaded to see. Webb's hand moved from the innocent and endearing stroking of the schoolgirl's calf, upwards, so that his wristwatch caught her red pleated skirt and lifted it slightly, at which point she turned to the window. She stepped across and pulled a cord to draw the curtains. There was a blankness in her eyes, in her face, no desire or passion so far as Gerry could see. Indeed she seemed in a daze, and Gerry stared up at her from his hiding place across the street without fear of discovery. The curtains slowly came across, were adjusted at the middle, and then left, still and heavy. Behind them, presumably, the girl returned to the sofa, to Webb's lascivious petting. Gerry, shut outside in a storm of abhorrence, a downpour of lust and jealousy, knew only one thing. This had to be stopped. Something must be done. The idea of Webb enjoying intercourse with this lovely young girl was unnatural, immoral, insufferable. Gerry must stop it for the sake of the girl, he must disabuse her of whatever Christian delusions Webb had instilled in her and free her from his clutches. And he must stop it for his own sake too, for he simply could not bear his imagination to be poisoned with these images. Webb had to meet himself. He had found a niche where nothing threatened his idea of who he was. He had surrounded himself with the uneducated, the under-confident, the penniless, and he stood so tall among them, administering his blessings. And – for goodness' sake! - administering his beatings! What would Jake make of this? Gerry was perhaps the only person there ever would be in his life who could possibly undo him. To go back now to Notting Hill with a basinful of this on his mind was unthinkable. He would kill someone. He would kill himself. He thought that he began to understand what it was to commit a crime of passion. He felt that he could kill. Yes, he could murder. The thing depended not on instability, on being temporarily unhinged or unbalanced. On the contrary, it depended on an exact balance. On the one side a personal recklessness, a genuine disregard for one's own life, and on the other an all-consuming desire for some abuse to stop.

My life, Gerry thought. *My life I rate at nothing!*

He came out from behind the tree, descended the wall, squeezed between the fat flanks of two German saloons, and walked briskly across the crescent to the steps of No. 3 Observatory Gdns. Without hesitation he went up the steps and found himself on a single, broad, flat and ancient flagstone, standing within the porch itself. All at once he felt supremely alert, each of his senses was at its peak. Some instinct had been disturbed within him that revitalized his ageing frame. He was nineteen again. He was about to throw the javelin sixty-eight yards for a college record. He looked about himself in an automatic way, with the reflexes of the hunter, the killer. The hunted, the killed. The road was empty. Suddenly he could see so very clearly the dimpled wetness on the tarmac, glistening under the lofty yellow street lamps; and the curtains in the window, beautifully lined with a diamond patterned satin. There was a small, ragged, blue plastic milk crate in the porch. The bell push sat in a brightly polished square of brass, worn by generations of visitors, by the reaching hands of generations of children, by nannies' hands, maids' hands, gentlemen's hands, by Thomas Cawley's hands, by milkmen's hands, and now by Gerry's small and murderous hand.

He did not know precisely what he would say but that did not concern him. He knew Webb would be dumbstruck to see him here, and from that moment Webb would know the game was up. He might try and slam the door in his face, of course. But whatever his reaction it would be the wrong one and it would be too late.

It was the Asian girl who answered the door, however. The golden clasp had been removed and her hair was undone and fell around her shoulders. One side of her jumper was slightly ruffled. Gerry looked down to her feet. They were bare. They were broad and perfectly formed. They were feet that had run on sand all childhood long.

"Yes?" she said. "Good evening."

On the warm air that tumbled out from the splendid house Gerry caught a trace of perfume, a soft scent of musk. He felt uncomfortable before this woman. Her Asian beauty and her perfect clothes, the crisp pleats of her red skirt, made him conscious once more of his own disgraceful appearance.

Good grief - whatever was he doing here?

He drew himself up. "Is Mr Alec Webb at home?"

"Alec," she called back - but it was not a call, just his name.

"Yes?"

"There's a gentleman here to see you."

In a second or two Webb emerged from the living room without his sweater, tucking in his white shirt. His shirt was unbuttoned, exposing his dark and wiry chest.

"Gerry!" he said, approaching the door. "What the heck - Come in! For goodness' sake!"

He gestured Gerry over the threshold and onto the deep, green carpet that overflowed from the living room into the hallway. Gerry did not move.

"What on earth brings you here?"

To Gerry's confusion there was no sign whatever of discomfiture about Webb's manner. He had been surprised, yes, but that was momentary, that had already passed, it was already irrelevant. He seemed not in the least bit anxious, guilty or afraid. He was full of bonhomie. Gerry, who had planned to take charge from the start, who had expected right now to be nodding, slowly and wisely, at a very nonplussed Alec Webb, or already to be hectoring the pair of them as they sat cowed on the sofa, instead found himself quite under-confident in the new surroundings of No. 3 Observatory Gdns. He was actually very ill at ease.

"What brings you here? Is something wrong? You look a little overwrought again, Gerry."

The lovely Asian girl moved slightly behind Webb. "Can I get you a drink?" she offered, sliding her hair behind her ear. The question, her movement and her demeanour all made her seem more like a servant than a companion to Webb, yet in his presence at least, neither appeared uncomfortable on account of that.

Gerry and Webb stared at each other.

"Get Gerry a drink, darling. Get him a gin. A stiff one. A belter. He looks all out of it."

There was a pause. Gerry thought he saw some faltering in Webb's eyes, but then Webb moved towards him and it was gone.

"Come on in, Gerry." The use of his name was overdone: Gerry was being patronized again. He was seen as someone weak, confused, infirm, again. Not quite all there, you know. Few cards short of a full deck. Lift doesn't quite get to the top any more, you know . . .

Gerry moved forward automatically and Webb slipped behind him and shut the door.

"Take off your jacket, Gerry. Is that possible, I wonder?" Webb chuckled amiably. Gerry was a guest who'd just arrived for Christmas Eve cocktails. "*Can* you take it off, old feller? Does it indeed come off? I don't believe I've ever seen you without this old faithful. It's a Harris Tweed, I betcha!" After removing the jacket Webb held it up to inspect the label on the sagging, yellowed, inside pocket. "I said so! There you are! Harris Tweed! By their tweeds ye shall know them!"

Webb was now ushering him towards the entrance of the living room and Gerry found himself stepping forward over the deep, green carpet, whose sponginess seemed to draw from him all power of volition. And here he was at the living room doorway, suddenly a part of the world he had been looking into from outside. There was the green sofa. There was the side table. There was the brass tray. What a transition to move from outside to inside. Webb was still behind him. Gerry turned back in time to see his host proffer his Harris Tweed to the Asian girl, and at the same time whisper something to her, something about "the one whose wife - "

Ah. So Webb had jumped to the conclusion that Gerry had come here on account of some news about his wife. Bad news, presumably, if the state of his guest were anything to go by. Perhaps Webb thought Gerry had come to seek guidance and sympathy in an hour of darkest need. No doubt that was the story the pastor was telling himself, and telling the lovely Asian girl too, of course. How very convenient. Until Gerry had relaxed and his thoughts had begun to run more freely (perhaps the gin would help) he decided that it would be best just to play along. For the moment he was clean out of initiative. But once he and Webb were talking he would gradually manoeuvre the conversation onto his terms. He would not be drawn into all this, fooled by all this - the luxury and the upper class courtesy, the ready gin and tonic. Oh no. He would keep a clear head and bide his time until he too had his wits properly about him. And though he was covering it well, surely Webb must feel some anxiety at having one of the dirty denizens of his other world come out here, sniff him out, push his bell, mess up his carpet.

"Sit down, Gerry."

Webb gestured to the sofa and brought round the armchair of the suite for himself, parking it so that it faced the sofa more directly. He was about to sit down when the Asian girl returned with Gerry's drink. He crossed quickly and took it from her and said something softly to her, too softly for Gerry to catch what it was. In response she turned and left the room and Webb closed the door behind her.

"So, Gerry," he said, returning and offering Gerry his drink, and taking his own in exchange from the brass tray. "To what do I owe this pleasure?"

Gerry took his gin and tonic and sipped it twice before putting it to rest on the tray. He detected a shift in his favour. With the girl out of the way Webb's courtesies were stiffer, more wooden.

"I expect you are rather surprised to see me," he said, a quiet challenge rising in his voice. He cleared his throat. Already the gin fumes had found their way beneath some mucus in his windpipe. He cleared his throat again, loudly, assertively.

"Were you not surprised?"

"Yes, of course - but has something happened, Gerry?" Webb ran a fingertip around the rim of his crystal tumbler. He had nowhere to put his drink. "Has there been some news?" he asked earnestly. "Regarding your wife? Have they found her? Is she all right, do you know?"

There was a pause. Then Gerry said simply:

"They've found her."

"And?"

A big idea had barged into Gerry's head, a big bully of

an idea, elbowing out all other considerations. If he went along with the pretence Webb had offered him, even embellished it a little, then could he not return to this afternoon's original objective, and ask Webb, while he was caught on the hop as it were, while his Christian sympathy was put to the test as it were, could he not ask him for the money he so urgently needed to go to Pwllheli? He could be on his way at dawn! Oh, a good plan! A bold plan. A neat plan. The other matters, personal matters, political matters, could surely wait. He had to rearrange things, re-prioritise, box clever. The ticket to Pwllheli had to be his uppermost concern. He reached for his gin and tonic, took another sip - what a heavenly drink! - and licked his lips. He felt some lengthy stubble around his mouth, which he'd rather not have reminded himself about just at this moment. He replaced his glass on the brass tray and sat back, settled into the sofa. He glanced about the room, taking in the furnishings, biding his time.

"Is she all right? Your wife?"

For a moment Gerry found himself at a loss to reply.

"Is she all right, Gerry? Your wife?"

"They've found her," he announced again, this time with the same gravitas as Detective Sergeant Tenmere.

"Well, this is excellent news. Wonderful news. For everyone. For all concerned. Thank heavens. But is she in good health? Did you say she was all right?"

Gerry checked Webb's phoney solicitations with some of D.S.Tenmere's rougher vernacular - "They've got her now. She's been running them ragged." He stopped and sipped again from his glass. "I'm quite proud of her in a way, you know. She's turned out to be a hard-nosed little operator. Worthy meat for our boys in blue." Why was he talking in this crude way? *Why*? The gin, the gin. But he took another sip! It was irresistible.

"Ah, she's well, then. I take it. Safe and sound."

Gerry nodded. "She's been holed up in North Wales."

"Really," Webb said. "I see."

Gerry leant forward. "Look Alec," he began. "I know you and I have not got along." He looked Webb straight in the eye. In response Webb's bald eyes narrowed with suspicion, but Gerry pressed on. He only had to hit the right note - frankness and humility, earthy Christian virtues. "I'm not pretending otherwise, Alec. I've been rude at times and downright bloody unpleasant to you."

"You certainly have, old boy."

"I've been a shit," Gerry confessed, nodding - but why such language! - "and that's the least of it. But you must see that that's not really the real me, the real Gerry Delaporte. I've not been myself lately. I think you know the reasons why well enough. I've shoved them down your throat once too often, haven't I? Haven't I?" Gerry chuckled lamely at that, but Webb offered no chuckle in return, no meeting, no reconciliation. "But here I am," Gerry pressed on, "up against it. Really up against it, Alec." He knew he was overusing the name, but he couldn't stop himself now, not when Webb stared back at him as if he knew exactly what was coming. "You've already been more than kind to me. From the first you've always treated me with generosity and respect. You took me out for lunch, remember? The first time we met. At *The Horse and Groom*. Steak and kidney pie!" He was gibbering. The drink. The gin. "I haven't forgotten, you see. And tonight you've welcomed me into your own home when could have just slammed the door in my face. Plenty would have done, in your position. It was what I half expected and God knows it's what I deserve." No response to that either. How far did he have to go? "But here I am in your house, on your sofa, drinking your very pleasant gin and tonic. Your G and T! Your Gin and It! And - " another chuckle, but still to no avail. Hopeless. This was hopeless. Webb's face was stone. "And to be perfectly honest, I have come to ask you a favour - that is, you see, beyond even the generosity you have already shown me." He had to press on: he could not allow any silence to open up in the green living room, over the green lake of carpet. "Now they've found my wife there's some hope at last. I must see her. Immediately. Obviously. That much is plain. I was wondering if you could possibly see your way clear to - "

"How did you find my address?"

"Pardon?"

"How did you know my address?"

"I - I overheard you give it to a cabbie. This afternoon. I was going to speak to you then. I was just approaching you to tell you about my wife - "

"Ah." Webb was gently stroking his cut crystal tumbler again. Now he looked down. "Ah," he said again, but differently, regretfully, as if realizing some careless slip which he had guarded against for a very long time.

"You see, the thing is, the thing is - " But Gerry had entirely lost his grip. He felt himself flush. Blood suffused his face in great throbs and waves. It was an agonizing feeling of exposure, of helplessness, as if he were wetting himself in front of Webb.

Webb finished his drink and got to his feet. He could really drink. He could really put it away. He strode over to the sofa and held out his hand. "Gin?"

Gerry was in such a state over the pig's ear he was making of this that he dared not drink any more. He hadn't touched alcohol for months and his metabolism simply could not deal with it. He was gibbering like an idiot.

"Er, no. No thanks."

Webb turned on his heel and went to the door. "Gin lives in the fridge," he called over his shoulder.

Gerry seized the opportunity to bury his face in his hands. Why could he not just come out with it? Why not? Why not? Because, of course, because . . . Gerry brought himself to think the unthinkable. That this God-fearing man, with all his wealth, was not prepared to lend him twenty-five pounds for a lousy rail ticket. Lend him, that was all. Oh no. Surely that could not be it. Surely he was just making him beg. He was forcing him to get down on his knees as an act of penance for all the insult he'd vomited up in the other world, in Notting Hill. Well, he would beg then. He would go through that, because with the cash in hand he could leave by the first train, at dawn, and his whole life could be transformed by lunch time. Surely such a prospect was worth some pride.

Webb returned, his glass replenished, a fresh twist of lemon suspended in the bubbles.

"Gerry," he began affably, taking his seat once more. "How would it be if I were to lend you my umbrella? Forecast said it's going to pour down. I can pick it up in the morning, if I'm passing that way." He took another large gulp of gin, set his glass on the carpet at his feet, crossed his legs, and knitted his hands together in his lap. "There's something I want to point out to you, Gerry. You're a man of some refinement, and I want to see if you noticed this. I want to test your powers of observation. When I asked you if you wanted another drink just now, what did I say, exactly?"

Gerry didn't know what to do. He had lost any purchase on the conversation.

"I don't know."

"Go on. Try and remember. It's important."

"I can't. I can't remember. More gin?"

151

"No! Wrong! Wrong wrong wrong, Gerry. And you such a man of refinement. Such a gentleman. No. That is not what I said at all, Gerry old chap. I said - and this is all I said - I said - *Gin*?"

"Look, Alec, I - "

"I said *Gin*? Because in the best households, in the best households, Gerry, one does not say, More gin? Or, 'Would you like another?' One does not say that." Webb was in full pastoral mode now. He sat with hands knitted in his lap, his odd monkish fringe in a perfect line across his forehead, and his silvery spectacles glinting in the soft light; light thrown by lamps all around the beautiful living room - standard lamps, grandfatherly heirlooms, widowers, proud, erect and alone, or table lamps, plump and grandmotherly, sitting on priceless lacquered cabinets, surrounded by figurines in jade and marble, everywhere you looked. Gerry didn't know what to do. He was in the young carpenter's position, John Fitzroy's position. He was the supplicant, the mendicant even, entirely at the mercy of the pastor.

"And why not, pray? Because it is rude. It could imply that you are secretly quantifying the consumption of your guest, when of course everything should be, as it were, his, or at least at his disposal, thus one should think of the gin bottle as just the gin bottle, or your guest's gin bottle, but not as your gin bottle, so that your guest alone is accountable for his consumption therefrom . . ."

The man was drunk. Gerry knew he had to seize the moment before all became irrecoverable. This was as good an opportunity as he was going to get. He just had to beg for it. Twenty-five pounds. A pony! He just had to eat the humble pie, and then Webb would fetch his wallet, drunk as he was, drunk as a lord, he'd fetch his wallet, open it, take out the notes, hand them over, and Gerry could be out of here in a couple of minutes.

"Alec. I'm sorry to interrupt your train of thought. This isn't easy for me, believe me."

"Yes?"

Webb suddenly looked entirely sober.

"I need to borrow the rail fare, Alec. The fare to Wales. To Pwllheli. Will you lend it to me? Please. A pony should cover it."

Behind his glasses Webb's bald eyes narrowed again.

"What in heaven's name is a pony, Gerry? You don't use the word in its usual sense."

"Alec. Can you lend me twenty-five pounds, please?"

Webb swallowed hard. He shook his head and repeated the figure faintly to himself. "Twenty-five pounds. My word. And that's a pony?"

How Gerry cursed himself for introducing this phoney pony slang, which belonged to neither of them. And at such a delicate juncture.

"We were talking about etiquette, Gerry, in a light-hearted way."

"I can pay it back to you straightaway. Perhaps even tomorrow evening."

"A pony, you say. Gerry . . ." Alec Webb sat back in his armchair and sighed. "Gerry. Old feller." He sighed again, as if he had to go right back to the beginning. "We were talking about something entirely different. Etiquette, I believe."

"I'm sorry." Gerry relaxed now that his request was out in the open. The words of humility, or of self-disparagement at least, flowed easily. "I know I'm rude. I know I'm crass, I'm gross, I'm coarse, I stink and I'm insufferable. I know, I know. And I wouldn't ask, I really wouldn't, only I'm desperate. You must see that. I know you can see that."

"Gerry." Webb's brow furrowed beneath the monkish fringe, an eyebrow lifted. "Gerry! Neither a borrower nor a lender be!"

"Oh for goodness' sake!" Gerry burst out. "Stop kidding me around!" He cast an arm around the living room. "With all this, you won't lend me twenty-five pounds? I don't believe it. You must be kidding! You must be!" Gerry chuckled again, but helplessly, hopelessly. "Come on! Pay up, man! I'll give it back tomorrow evening. On the nail!" He slapped his thigh but the sound died immediately, swallowed by the lush green carpet.

Then he said it.

"I am begging you."

And on saying it the words found their own tone, their own quiet and quivering humility. It was no sham, no pretence. He knitted his hands together in the gesture of the mendicant. He shuffled forward on the sofa. He dropped to his knees on the carpet.

"I am begging you."

Alec Webb sat back again in his chair but now his mouth was tight and his head shook resolutely. "I don't believe in it. Never have done." He spoke now on some matter of pride, of honour even, family honour. "It disgusts me."

Gerry undid his hands, felt behind him for the sofa's edge with trembling fingers. What had he done? What was he doing? He raised himself, one haunch at a time, back onto the sofa, back into the seat.

"You mean you really won't lend it to me? You won't lend me anything? Not twenty-five pounds? When I'm begging you. I can't believe this."

"I'd like to, Gerry. Believe me. But I can't. It would be easy, more than easy. It would be a pleasure, in fact. But I can't. I must resist the temptation. If one has a principle in life, one must stand by it."

There was a silence. Gerry grunted. The tension lifted. He had his answer. He set his arm along the back of the sofa and stared hard at Alec Webb. His stubbled upper lip quivered with feeling: "Why, you tight-arsed Christian shite! You hypocritical - "

But there was an explosion from Webb. He leapt to his feet, drunkenly knocking over his glass and casting a dark, vulgar tongue across the green carpet, ulcerated at its tip with lemon rind.

"NO!" he cried. "Not here, my friend! You are speaking to Sir Alec Webb, in his own house!"

Webb towered over him, his eyes blazing behind his spectacles. Anger and drink inflamed his ugliness, his lips swelled and trembled.

"You really are a *maggot*, Mr Delaporte, do you know that? A self-pitying little maggot! Do you think I care what you think?" Webb's voice had a high strain Gerry had never heard before, something needling, almost theatrical. "I know how your petty mind works! I've seen it all before. You don't understand that all this - " he swept an arm around the room - "doesn't matter!" He shook his head. "It doesn't matter. It's just things. I'm the same man, doing the same job. The answer is no, Mr Delaporte. I'd not give away a silver teaspoon of any of this. You can't solve people's problems by throwing money at them." He stepped closer, as if thrust on by some new, provoking thought. "To think that I gave up my taxes for you and your kind! Never enough, though, is it? And if you can't get it from me you'll be down the social security first thing in the morning trying to scrounge it from them!" That idea made him lose patience altogether. "You're a washout, Delaporte! A washout of the first water! Get out of here! Get out of my house! You have no welfare rights here! You are not the landlord here! Get out! Get on your bike! *Get out!*"

Leaving Gerry no chance to respond, Webb stooped and caught hold of his arm from the back of the sofa and dragged him up. He whipped Gerry's arm behind his back, drawing a faint cry from Gerry -

"No need for this . . ."

Webb frogmarched him out to the front door.

"Open the door, Gentleman Gerry!"

Obediently Gerry opened the front door, his free hand fumbling with the heavy brass latch. Webb thrust him out with such force he slipped and staggered down all eight steps, only just keeping his balance.

It was raining. As the forecast had said. And he had no umbrella.

"Here!" Webb called from the top of the steps. He tossed down Gerry's Harris Tweed. The Nicholson's Streetfinder came out the side pocket and fell in the wet.

Webb slammed shut his front door.

Chapter Eleven

Ticket to Ride

"I require you to expedite the payment as soon as possible. Immediately, in fact, in view of the circumstances."

Gerry's voice was muffled by a cold, but in the subdued and smoky atmosphere of the social security offices his diction set queues turning, heads nodding, mouths muttering. He was something to look at too. He'd slept little and was very much the worse for wear. Some of the clothes he'd worn in the rain the previous evening he'd had to put on again, still in their damp condition, to come down here. He was uncomfortable, irritable, dishevelled, altogether at a low ebb.

"Swallowed a dictionary, have we?"

The clerk, an old adversary of Gerry's here, an obese young woman with blue oval glasses, slipped off her stool, adjusted her skirts, and walked away with his letter from D.S.Tenmere. Gerry's view through the window was obscured by some grubby plywood masking, but by putting his head to the glass and peering after her he could see her stop to chat with a fellow clerk, two queues down. This was a new woman, a Scot, sour looking, with a dark dry perm. Gerry had so far been careful to avoid this Scot.

"Little Lorrd Fontlerroy, ay prresume?"

She said it without lifting her head from her forms.

The obese clerk waved the letter and passed on.

"He only wants a rail fare to some holiday resort in Wales."

"Firrst-class, o'courrse."

Gerry's clerk sidled on between the crowded desks, dislodging files here and there with her voluminous skirts.

The queue behind Gerry, as soon as it was seen that the clerk had gone walkabout, had disappeared. He stood on his own. He waited there a full fifteen minutes, shifting from hip to hip. There was a troubling stiffness in his right hip and to relieve it he leant to his left, but now the left ached also. The first pains of arthritis, perhaps. He had always enjoyed such good health, despite the pressure and anxiety of his working life, but since falling to his current depths he'd noticed poor bowel habits, itching gums, scalp disorders, eyes failing - the whole machine wearing out and giving up. It had had enough, even if he were game for more.

At last the clerk returned. She had in her hand a large mug of coffee heavily lip-sticked about the rim. On it was printed, in a saucy script, *"I like it just as it comes!"*

"You'll have to sit down and wait."

She brought the cup to her lips and took a sip. She did not sit down herself and kept her eyes lowered on someone else's papers.

"They're dealing with it," she added, when Gerry did not move.

This was as much as he could hope for. He turned away to find the queue pressing behind him again. He squeezed his way through to a row of dirty orange chairs at the back of the room, and parked himself near the tannoy, knowing how infernally difficult it could be to hear what was said.

"I like it just as it comes!"

That lewd ambiguity. So open, so blunt, so funny, presumably. A young person's sexual desire advertised on the side of her coffee mug. It was the car sticker mentality, of course. The rear window, or bumper sticker mentality that had ushered in a new golden age of innuendo and explicitness. This kind of thing had even made its way into the staff car park at school, imported by a P.E. teacher. Not a young man, in fact. A family man in his forties, a returnee from insurance broking. On the back of his rusty Austin Maxi was: "Rugby is a game for men with odd shaped balls!" With that the green light had been given. Faddish Molly Saunders from Home Economics decorated the rear window of her Nissan Cherry: "Windsurfers do it standing up!" In the same spirit his old enemy here, this obese young woman with blue oval glasses, had bought this mug and brought it here, to her place of work. Look at my mug. Read my mug. 'I want sex. I like sex'. Like Mik and Kim, openly abandoning themselves to their noisy, their raucous lust. For Gerry it had always been and always would be the other way about. He could no more make light of his cravings, no more joke about his sex organs, than he could play rugby or windsurf. He'd been brought up with a few taboos, for better or worse.

A *Daily Mirror*, folded on the next seat, declared: **I DID IT!** Gerry took the paper. I did what? A drunken celebrity in evening dress stumbled from a nightclub -

"Mr Delaporte! Mr Delaporte! Booth seventeen. Mr Delaporte! Booth seventeen!"

Gerry folded and replaced the paper and went to the screened area of private booths.

"Mr Delaporte!"

All right, all right. I'm coming.

"Mr Delaporte! Booth seventeen!"

Gerry found the booth in time to stop the young man calling his name out a sixth time. With a disappointed air, the clerk - who had the very face of facelessness: long and gaunt, with square rimless glasses - pushed the microphone away and picked up Gerry's letter from the police. Paper-clipped to it now were several other, smaller papers, evidence of other hands all busily engaged in their light, tedious, meaningless tasks, passing bucks and coffee mugs to and fro. Uppermost of these documents was a typed and official looking memorandum on yellow paper. The young man interpreted aloud this document for Gerry, laying a special emphasis, for reasons of his own, on the repetitive use of the word 'ticket' in the text, which seemed to offend him. He glanced up at Gerry and offered a thin lipped smile each time he used the word.

"The *ticket*, which is a return *ticket*, will be available for your collection from the enquiries desk at Euston station after ten o'clock this morning. The *ticket* cost will be deducted from your forthcoming benefit. The first possible train for you is at ten-twenty, which gets into Birmingham New Street at twelve-o-five. From there you'd catch the twelve-twenty to Holyhead, via Bangor, which arrives at, er - " a moment's doubt over the slowness of this train - "which gets in at Bangor, as I said, at, er, at two-thirty-five. But you can check the connections or alternative trains when collecting your *ticket*. How does all that suit you, Mr Delaporte? Does it suit you very well?"

"Very well indeed," Gerry replied, ignoring the young man's superciliousness. "Is there anyone in particular with whom I am to liaise at Euston station?"

"Is there anyone in particular with whom you are to liaise?" the young clerk repeated, frowning, perplexed by the question. Then he answered it: "There is indeed, Mr Delaporte. There is a Mr Barrington. Liaise, by all means, with Mr Barrington about your *ticket*. At the *ticket* enquiries desk, as I said."

Gerry pressed on, anxious to avoid any further sparring.

"Please notify the police of these arrangements so that they can inform their opposite numbers in Pwllheli."

"Ah. I cannot do that for you, Mr Delaporte, I'm afraid."

The clerk's disappointed air returned. He shook his head and sighed regretfully. Oh, the obvious pleasure it gave him to introduce new difficulties. Good heavens, the tedium of ordinary working lives! The vast, sad waste of precious time. Of hours and days and weeks and years. At least that bit was over, that everlasting stupidity. Only the sense of its utter fatuousness remained.

The clerk detached the memorandum from his other documents and passed it across. Gerry took up the yellow paper, folded it, and put it away in the inside pocket of his Harris Tweed. He hesitated, then decided to risk the obvious question.

"Well, why can't you do that?"

"I'm afraid our responsibility ends here, Mr Delaporte," the clerk continued, adjusting his paper clip. "It is down to you to notify the police. It is in your interest alone, you see. That information has to come first-hand from you, otherwise any setback arising may be attributable to ourselves. We have no further administrative role in a case of this kind. Good day to you, Mr Delaporte." He stood up before Gerry could do so and looked down at him, scoring some further point with his surprising, dangling height. "Have a nice trip." His eyebrows arched above his glasses and his lips sealed tight on that last word 'trip'.

Lingering a few moments in booth seventeen after the clerk had gone, Gerry allowed himself for the first time to enjoy the thought that things were in motion now, plans were afoot - bugger the supercilious clerk, he did not matter, of what relevance was he now? Within a few hours, half a day at the most, Gerry would again be face to face with his wife, whom he had not seen for more than four months but whom, prior to that, he had seen continuously, on a day-to-day basis, for more than thirty years. This meeting later today - later today! - would change his life as no other meeting ever had done nor ever could. He need never have cause to visit these offices, these people, again. But what about Anna herself? Could he say, in all honesty, that he had missed her? Missed her wit and conversation, perhaps? No. She had had none. And he had not missed her sympathy, not even in his darkest hours. At those particular times he would have welcomed her presence least of all. She had not the slightest understanding of his innermost feelings. Had he missed her physically, then? Bodily? No. Not for a moment. As no doubt she had not missed him. His absence in that regard could have been nothing but a guilty relief. Strange how these awful truths had outgrown their usefulness, though. They need not be spoken of now. Separation itself had proved these things beyond any doubt, and had made speaking of them quite pointless.

On his way to the police station in Ladbroke Grove, there to finalise his arrangements with Detective Sergeant Tenmere, C.I.D., it struck Gerry as very healthy to be thinking of his wife like this, in this rather cold and brutal way. How much better it felt to allow his bitterness to flow freely in its own broad channels, rather than to force it back into the convoluted guttering of his old manners and sympathies. To take such a hard line made him feel self-sufficient and resolved, a man with a mission, and this sense of purpose distracted him from morose reflections on the events of the previous evening. There was a rail ticket as good as in his back pocket and he was about to reclaim all that was rightfully his. From this perspective the humiliating failure at Observatory Gdns. was of no account.

But what a strange business that had been too. Webb had not come out of it so cleanly either. Far from it. He had rather lost control. Gerry could well imagine Webb kicking himself now for drinking so much and laying himself so bare. Sir Alec Webb, indeed. He would get hold of a Debrett's and check that out. Or could he really be bothered? Such things seemed so irrelevant when he thought of the captivatingly beautiful girl – was she a Thai? Just another poor little sex slave from that desperate, prostituted country? What a national shame to have your daughters couple with the likes of Alec Webb! That blank look in her eyes as she drew the curtains in preparation for Webb's postprandial seduction. Was it a nightly ritual, this? Judging from her automated responses it could easily have been.

Gerry's pace stiffened as he considered the awful mismatch of her delicate and lovely frame with the coarse and hairy, blubber-lipped Englishman. It was too grotesque to contemplate. Couldn't Webb see that nature, let alone God, never intended such a match? It was monstrous, it was inhuman. To think of Webb's gross penis penetrating her, working its way into her, doubtless causing her excruciating pain while he enjoyed his delicious satisfaction - could Webb not see that this was improper, bestial? Or was that part of the sadistic eroticism? The sylph-like size of the girl and her demure and subservient attitude made the relationship much like that between father and daughter: there was something of the corruption of incest about Webb's lust, and the bestiality of the paedophile. Yet Webb lived on protected, by his position, his wealth, the very way he spoke. Impervious. Somehow he must be stopped. It was all too much to let pass, to contemplate.

Gerry wondered idly what the full story was. Were there parents-in-law still living? What had they thought of the match? What had they thought of this ugly and ungainly Englishman picking their daughter out the gutter and carrying her off to his hotel, where he could fatten her up into a sex object, marvellously pretending it was all an act of Christian mercy? Gerry resolved that as soon as he was on his feet financially he would do something about Webb's iniquitous delusions, beginning with the plight of this third-world child-bride.

The fantasy popped into his head that he might perform some act of rescue. He might abduct her himself! And why not? A return to chivalry! He would take her to Provence and they would live platonically there. What a very intoxicating idea this was - Good heavens, how it stirred him! How things could change and change about, if one just had a bit of money. Yes, they would live platonically there, in Provence. Eventually, perhaps, it would be his honour to give her away to some civilized Frenchman. By then he would have taught her French: they would have their lessons on the balcony after lunch, with some cheese and olives and the last of the wine. The young couple would wed in a broken-down church in the valley of the Durance. He knew the very place. There would be photographs among the olive groves. There would be the most magnificent reception. He would cook the more involved dishes himself, but he would also manage the caterers with a rod of iron, oh yes, doing the rounds of dipping and tasting, careful not to drop sauce on his morning suit . . . And through the balm of this more natural union the wounds Alec Webb had left on the poor girl's body and mind would slowly heal. She would forget the awful Christian guilt and all the tacit blackmail, the gross sexual favours and demands, and Webb's repulsive, dangling body. Gerry would be a new father to her, and the kindest, most indulgent father imaginable. What a pleasurable idea that was, suddenly, to be a father. He had never really wanted children before. There had been a period, of course, when he and Anna had left it to chance, but nothing had resulted and neither had been particularly bothered or upset. Indeed, they'd both felt a guilty relief about their childlessness. And then, as the hormones receded and life filled up with the sickness of work and the convalescence of holidays, there seemed less and less room for babies, and the thought of starting a family became quite ludicrous. Hadn't they problems enough? But for Gerry now, in comfortable retirement on his own, the prospect of taking on a ward of this kind would be a different matter. It would stir a love and vitality within him he had not known before. And who knows, in his village in Provence, there might be some widow of his age, or younger, whom he might meet at le poste from time to time, or at the sunny, breezy market there, and one day a conversation might begin, quite innocently perhaps, about the price of pears or artichokes, which led easily from one thread to another until it transpired they shared a common love of –

Chapter Twelve

Len Barrington

"I should like to see a Mr Barrington. I am expected. Mr Barrington has a ticket for my collection."

"Mr Barrington, sir?"

"That is correct."

"Are you sure, sir?"

"Perfectly sure."

"One moment, sir."

The young clerk, a lad in his teens, left the enquiries counter and went through a glass panelled door to the rear of the office. Gerry wanted to sit down. He had done quite enough standing around at counters for one morning. However, there were no seats in the enquiries' office and he was obliged to wait where he was.

A minute or so passed and then the youth reappeared the other side of the door, but he did not open it. An elderly man stood next to him, a man so short that only his head was visible, framed in the glass below the youth's, as if they stood poised for a family portrait, grandfather and grandson. The old man had a head of oily white hair and a short moustache which was white also, but browned about the nostrils with nicotine stains. His face was crimped with anxiety. His eyes, blue slits under fatty lids, shifted restlessly behind the glass, searching the enquiries' office for some enemy that threatened him out there. It was not Gerry. For some reason he could not see Gerry Delaporte, despite the youth's earnest efforts to point him out. The old man's face poked this way and that, following the youth's directions, but his anxious eyes would not, or could not, light on the particular member of the public who had asked to see him. Suddenly his head bobbed out of sight and the youth, after an eyes-up, apologetic glance, darted after him.

What new complication was this?

Both youth and old man came back and again the white head twisted about on its invisible neck, peering this way and that. Gerry took a couple of steps to his left, moving into the range of vision the old man seemed to prefer, but as soon as he had done so the man's anxious, tearful eyes focused directly ahead at where he had been standing a moment before. Gerry glanced at the clock. Nearly five past ten. He had done well to get himself here in good time for the first train and he didn't care to waste five minutes playing peekaboo. The other side of the glass the youth raised his hands in a gesture of helplessness. Apparently he couldn't persuade Mr Barrington to enter the enquiries' office! Dear oh dear. Whatever next. Gerry signalled the clerk to come back, and as he re-entered the old man bobbed out of sight again.

"Len!" the youth called after him, embarrassed and irritated by his colleague's behaviour.

But there was no response. He returned to the counter alone.

"Is that Mr Barrington?"

"That's Len Barrington, yes sir," the youth said. He leant forward and Gerry could smell his young breath, already stale with morning coffee and talk of timetables. "Between you and me, sir, Mr Barrington is not quite himself. He used to work out here, at this counter, until a few months ago. But he had some kind of breakdown. They've only just got him back to work. Agoraphobia?"

"But he's a public servant!" Gerry grunted. "Just my luck." He sighed and glanced again at the glass panel in the office door. "Look," he said to the young clerk, "I'm sorry about whatever it was, or is, that ails Mr Barrington, and I wish him a speedy recovery. However, all that I require is the ticket which the social security arranged for me to collect here this morning. Do you think you could get that from him and bring it through? Perhaps it's on his desk?"

Gerry did not want to be short with this youth, whose manner he found courteous and agreeable, and he was not accustomed to being treated with such deference of late. What a pleasant change from the oddballs at the social security offices.

"I'll see if it's there, sir."

The youth went back through the glass panelled door.

Gerry saw him go off to his right, as he had done before. After about a minute Len Barrington himself returned, but on his own. He stared through the glass again but this time his gaze was steady and direct, and he met Gerry's eyes without fear. He was smoking a cigarette which he brought to his lips. The smoke trickled from his nostrils and down through the tarred moustache. Then something mysterious happened. He nodded thoughtfully at Gerry, once, twice, as if recognizing him, placing him in some long lost context. Then, slowly and smokily, with deliberation, he mouthed something to Gerry through the glass.

"I . . . know . . . you . . . some . . . place . . ."

In response Gerry shifted impatiently on his sore hips. He refused to be perplexed or thrown by the experience in any way. Suddenly the youth was there again and he all but pushed Len Barrington aside. The door opened on a heated exchange between them, which ended with the clerk whispering hoarsely and very audibly to Barrington:

"Oh shove off, Len! You're about as much use around here as a wet fart!"

"What!?" Barrington barked back. "You young tosser! I'll teach you! I'll fix you! . . ."

The door closed and the youth came back to the counter with a purse-lipped smile.

"Sorry about that, sir. Little confusion. It was on Mr Barrington's desk all the time. Everything's in order. Would you sign for the ticket here, sir?"

Attached to the ticket was a form and a cross marked the place for Gerry to sign. The young man offered him a pen. At last the business was over and Gerry had the ticket safely in his hands. Bravo! He thanked the youth and left the enquiries' office without further delay.

He still had the ticket in his hand. He stopped and put it away safely in his inside pocket. He bought a *Guardian* at the news stand and was tempted to move on from there to a cup of tea and a croissant from one of the station buffets, but he decided to conserve the last of his meagre funds for a royal cooked breakfast on the train. He needed a treat to look forward to on what promised to be a long and tedious journey.

Chapter Thirteen

Bangor

A good-natured guard woke him when the train pulled in at Bangor station. He'd already been woken twice on the journey: once for his ticket shortly after leaving Euston, and again when changing trains at the bleak and alienating Birmingham New Street, where he'd had to switch from his luxury Inter-City to the sluggish and chilly branch-line service to Anglesey and Holyhead. Despite the inferior comfort of the branch-line carriage, Gerry had sunk into another slumber, and so deep this time that the guard at Bangor had to shake him to wake him up. If the guard had not bothered, he might have been shunted off across the bridge to Anglesey.

"Come along there, sir! Come along! For goodness' sake, sir! . . . Let's be having you! Come along!"

Gerry edged away from the guard's grip, which had become a forceful pinch. He'd never felt worse. Every limb was wrung by some virulent ague. He dragged his body out from the seat as if it were not part of him, as if it were the body of a reluctant dog straining against the leash. He had not wanted sleep. He had wanted to sit and watch the views of the silent countryside, and to read his newspaper, and to eat a royal cooked breakfast in the buffet car, but all such pleasures had flicked by him, like the first miles of telegraph poles, and he'd enjoyed nothing of his journey.

And now he was in Wales. North Wales. He was in historic Bangor. Was it possible? Once off the train he faced an endless platform that led to a flight of innumerable steps. Steps constructed from Welsh concrete by Welsh labourers, Welsh slaves, decades ago, when he was a child, and all those men were now dead, fallen, poor souls, while he soldiered on towards their steps. All around him there were bright green signs for toilets, trolleys, platforms, for tourist information, in both English and Welsh. They were too bright, too white and green, too new and garish and unfamiliar. He'd come out just a little too far today, strayed away from his routes to the library, the shops, West Kensington, the Kensington Palace side of things, just a little too far. He could not absorb such change. While he'd slept on the train something had drained out of him, all the confidence and resolution had leaked away and left nothing but a dark hollow, within which the freezing draughts of doubt, depression and alienation swirled, his three sisters chorusing, hissing, whispering and tittering, like tinnitus, the tuneless wind-chimes of madness. It was half a mile or more to the ticket barrier, a whole mile or more, and then there were the innumerable steps. He could make no progress. A pretty girl rushed by him, knocked him with her carrier bag. She turned a moment but said nothing. Warm brown eyes, like Kim. But she rushed on. The ticket barrier was a distant mirage thrown up by the acres of freezing concrete. Scraping trolley wheels jarred and jammed all around him. An electric cart beeped and whirred past. Where had the morning's mood gone? Some awful dream had sucked it away and abandoned him here. And there was no trace of that dream. Nothing. Nothing to worry at and cling to and try to understand. Nothing.

How absurd to imagine there would be any officer to meet him, as arranged with D.S.Tenmere, C.I.D., of Ladbroke Grove, two hundred odd miles away. He was coming to depend more and more on the services of the state. The social security. The police. Next would be the doctors and the hospitals.

The hospitals. And the doctor, in his white coat, on his rounds; the nurse taking his temperature, the orderly bringing tea. The doctor, obliged at all times to be smiling, tolerant, sympathetic, would settle a moment on his bedside, perch there, in big horn-rimmed glasses, a wise owl. And in no time Gerry would be the ward favourite, the one who brightened up the doctor's rounds with some wit and intellectual stimulation. The good doctor would turn out to be a fellow Francophile. "And how are we today, Monsieur Delaporte?" They would chat about Provence - in French, perhaps. Gerry offering a correction here and there, and the odd Provençal idiom. They'd discuss the price of property, of course. Oh, Gerry would admit, chuckling, he could never have dreamt of the kind of place the doctor and his family had in mind - not in a thousand years! - but even so he had enough put by, he thought, for a modest property *à la campagne* –

He would collapse at the foot of the concrete steps of

Bangor railway station and curl up into a ball, like some destitute drunkard, and wait for them here, the emergency services, the pretty women in funny hats who would come to tend him, on the concrete, with their gentle swabs and merciful needles.

But Gerry had it all wrong, all wrong. When he finally shuffled up to the ticket barrier there *was* someone waiting for him. A bearded bobby in full uniform, including a magnificently shiny peaked driving cap, stepped forward to greet him, offering a gloved hand for support.

"Mr Delaporte?"

His loathsome name. Loathsome. Monsieur Delaporte, don't you mean?

Gerry tried to say something but coughed so hard he gave it up.

"That's a nasty cough you've got there, sir."

The Welsh voice, soft and mellifluous, seemed to Gerry on the point of lifting into song. He wanted to bless this policeman. He wanted to say, 'God bless and keep you, constable'. The policeman stepped closer, a solicitous frown pulling down the peak of his shiny cap.

Gerry coughed again.

"That really is a nasty cough, sir. We'd better get you to the nick and whistle up some tea, sir."

Well, what a turn up for the books this was! It really was. Gerry could do nothing but mutter his thanks as the officer gently guided him to the steps. Without any hesitation or awkwardness, this kind young man tucked one hand under Gerry's arm, into the discoloured armpit of the ancient Harris Tweed, and helped him up the impassable, innumerable steps. Gerry would have preferred the policeman to put his arm all the way around him, and embrace him, and support him more fully. He felt so weak. He tried to remember when and what he had last eaten. A sausage roll was the last thing to pass his lips. He had bought it at an A1 Bakery on the way to Ladbroke Grove police station. He'd fallen asleep before he'd had a chance to buy the royal cooked breakfast on the Inter-City, and the Bangor train had had no buffet car, nor a toilet, nor any kind of creature comfort.

There was a short concourse when they reached the top of the steps and then a taxi rank in the open air. It was a mild, grey afternoon. "Looks like rain," the constable said cheerily, glancing up at the sky, as if rain was something he and his countrymen had long looked forward to. At the end of the taxi rank was parked a navy blue Volvo police car, with a second uniformed officer already in the driver's seat. Gerry raised his eyebrows at the handsome vehicle. It was for him? It couldn't be! Was he not to be directed up some boulder-strewn mountain path, or asked to ford the turbulence of a Celtic brook? Things were looking up, indeed! He had arrived at the final stage of this dreadful business, and not a moment too soon. There was nothing further to worry about or fear, after all.

It was Anna who had something to worry about now, something to fear. Oh yes. The time of reckoning was upon her.

The bearded officer opened the rear door and Gerry climbed into the Volvo. The door was shut behind him and he was cocooned in the car's dark comfort. Dry air from the heater caused a tickle in his throat, but he kept back his cough. It would have been unseemly to spill his germs here, right behind his police escorts, in their magnificent Volvo.

As they pulled away Gerry noted one or two suspicious, distasteful glances from the driver in the rear view mirror, but he felt that he quite understood these glances, and was at ease with them. When all was said and done he looked like nothing more than a wheezy tramp, who might have come from anywhere, been anywhere, who was the host for all kinds of parasites and fleas that would lay their eggs deep in the carpets of the Volvo, and those eggs would hatch out in the car's warmth, and all manner of bugs and mites would infest the carpets, and rise to bite and feed on the driver's ankles for months or years to come. Oh yes, it was quite understandable that the driver should be wary. He was part of a civilization that had laboured long and hard against the trials and persecutions of mother nature in order to produce this marvellous piece of machinery, over which he sat in magisterial command. Then into the back seat is dumped this outcast, this sack of filthy, stinking rags, infested with all the pests and nastinesses that it had taken so many centuries of ingenuity to rise above or destroy. Yes, Gerry could understand very well how he was perceived, and, true gentleman that he was, he was far too appreciative of all this warmth and comfort, given gratis, to bear any grudge.

After some busy, narrow streets around the station, the Volvo slipped through the town centre, ascended a hill of pre-war semis, and pulled into the car park of a low, modern, flat-roofed building of beige brick. Gerry was confused to find himself taken to Bangor rather than Pwllheli Police Station, but assumed there were good reasons, probably connected with D.S.Tenmere's 'protocol', to explain the diversion. It was a question of the nature of the case, no doubt, the size of the station, the rank of its commanding officer, and so on.

He was escorted swiftly inside and past the main desk, much to the alarm of the Desk Sergeant who raised a hand to stop his party in its tracks - "Oi! I've got to sort out a room yet!" he called after them, but in friendly fashion.

"In a minute, Ted!" the bearded constable shouted back

over his shoulder. "Don't mind him," he confided to Gerry. "He's such an old woman, old fusspot."

On either side of the corridor they passed a series of interview rooms, all with their doors ajar, all empty. They stopped at the furthermost one on the right. Gerry was asked to remain in this last room for the time being. A cup of tea would be on its way.

Well, this was all very promising. Gerry made a mental note to pay tribute to these officers before he left. He would perhaps seek out their superior and have a quiet word to commend the men to him. Yes, he would definitely do that.

The tea arrived promptly, served by the kinder of his two escorts, and with the tea was a side plate of biscuits. Bourbons, custard creams, wafers, Garibaldi. A respectable selection by any standard. When his attentive officer had gone, Gerry couldn't stop himself reflecting, with some gall, after a sip of tea and a nibble of Garibaldi, that the police did all right for themselves. Teachers had to buy their own tea and biscuits, and wash up their own mugs. No canteen for them. And his classroom had never been as warm as this in winter, and it had never been so clean and well painted and maintained, he thought, glancing around the bright linoleum and the freshly glossed skirting.

There was a soft, stroking knock on the door. The bearded constable reappeared, but he was only holding the door open for another officer.

This second policeman was, to Gerry, at first glance, quite shocking, quite unreal. He was a man of freakish, even frightening bulk, large enough actually to fill the doorway he stood behind, so that access to the interview room looked impossible. He was dressed up in some specially tailored High & Mighty, grey-green suit, the jacket of which was fastened at the middle by a single button. Gerry's bearded escort appeared suddenly wizened, gnomish beside this figure, not only physically but spiritually cowed, and this made his superior all the more threatening.

On a confidential nod from the officer the constable scurried away without a word. The timing was unnatural, as if the officer did not want his junior to see his next move, which was to glide through the doorway as if by legerdemain, executing such a deft manoeuvre he somehow avoided contact between body and door-frame. From his seat Gerry stared in awe and fascination, not daring to sip his tea or touch his biscuits.

The officer closed the door behind him and turned to face Gerry. His face was quite normal, even rather finely featured, and his hair was fair and rolled back from his brow in well groomed curls. But his neck hung apologetically about his jaw-bone (a barely discernible crease in the skin) so that there was no taper, just a shovel of flesh, the width of his jowls, which entirely covered his collar and the knot of his tie. He approached the table. He was a gross and intimidating spectacle, and he knew it. In his presence Gerry felt the outcome of the interview was a foregone conclusion. Doubtless many criminals had felt the same as he approached them.

When the officer pulled out his chair and sat down opposite, Gerry expected the floor boards beneath the linoleum to protest under the strain of such weight, but the floor was uncomplaining concrete. The officer looked down a moment, as if waiting for his chair to betray him. Then he went through a performance, tucking up the slack of his trousers about his thighs so the creases of his suit wouldn't spoil. How could a man like this worry about such a detail? These rituals completed, the officer looked into Gerry's face, focusing not on his eyes but on a point just above them, as if Gerry had a Cyclopean eye mid-forehead. Gerry found this disconcerting and appreciated that he was probably meant to, nonetheless he looked straight back into the officer's eyes, which were sagging, rheumy items, quite out of reach of his body's circulation.

"I am in charge of your case. I am Detective Sergeant Aldwich."

His voice was light and soft, almost a treble, almost that of a eunuch. His rank – such a source of pride to D.S.Tenmere – seemed a source of shame to Aldwich. He'd offered it with a touch of irony, as if it were an accepted understatement for some much more onerous position, a title that was perhaps at best irrelevant.

"Detective Sergeant Tenmere of Notting Hill C.I.D. updated me on your case over the telephone this morning." He paused. When he spoke again his voice was quiet and confidential. "I am afraid this is one of the most unpleasant duties I have to discharge, Mr Delaporte." But he stalled again, still unable to broach his news, and offered this aside: "D.S. Tenmere and I go back a long way, but he's left me in it this time - old Tenpence! - I have to admit!" He laughed shortly, sadly, resignedly. "I have to give you some very bad news, sir. Some very, very bad news."

All right, all right, Gerry wanted to say. Get on with it, please! Why were all these policemen so theatrical? Too much television.

Detective Sergeant Aldwich jutted out his jaw but the shovel of flesh beneath his chin retained its shape, still covered the tie knot, the jawbone merely taking up some slack. For a moment the officer's eyes met Gerry's, but then reluctantly lifted again to that spot mid-forehead, as if their tiny upward motion were governed by some internal counterweight. Gerry didn't feel it was his place to speak just yet. He didn't know if the officer could detect it in his

Cyclopean eye, but Gerry could not envisage any news that would be particularly distressing, unless it were that Anna had spent all his money.

"The news is very, very bad, sir, and it is my duty, as I say, to discharge."

"What on earth has happened, officer?"

"It concerns your wife, sir."

They were interrupted by a knock at the door. The door was opened in haste. It was the bearded constable once more. He looked exceedingly uncomfortable. He rolled his eyes skyward in exaggerated apology.

"Sorry, sarge ... Wrong room."

Detective Sergeant Aldwich turned and looked up at the constable. There was silence. Aldwich's expression became strained. Traces of colour struggled to the surface of his neck and cheeks. Saying nothing further to Gerry, who was suddenly forgotten, the officer stood and went to the door. Gerry watched for the deft manoeuvre which would enable him to exit the interview room. He saw it. A disguised swing of the hips took the trunk sideways, allowing the detective - head dipped momentarily - passage to the other side. He slammed the door behind him with such force flakes of the fresh gloss fell from the architrave.

"You are in for a bollocking, my son."

He may as well not have closed the door his voice was so clear and loud. Gerry heard the two policemen start back down the corridor together. The Detective Sergeant continued to berate the constable, and Gerry was able to follow every word, as indeed every other person in the police station must have been able to. "A bollocking. I am not amused. I am not amused."

It was another quarter of an hour before anyone crossed the threshold of Gerry's interview room again. His teacup was dry and stained and just a few brown crumbs remained on the side plate where the biscuits had been. After the noisy bollocking in the corridor, there had been other noises in and around the police station which Gerry, confined to his room and with nothing else to distract his attention, had tried hard to follow. There had been many angry voices, the loudest and most angry of which had been that of Detective Sergeant Aldwich himself. When he got going everyone else stopped. The police station had become a hotbed of recrimination, with everyone blaming each other for some inexcusable cock-up. No other business seemed to concern any of the officers on duty. The angry conversations were punctuated by various doors banging and, occasionally, by a pair of angry feet marching down the corridor outside Gerry's room, accompanied by some muttering under the breath, sorrowful or angry, which Gerry could not make out. As far as he could tell the entire police station, the whole flat-roofed, flat-footed building, on its hill of pre-war semis, was now in angry uproar, with doors banging, boots stamping, desk counters slamming down all around the place. But no matter how he strained Gerry could snatch nothing intelligible from the exchanges beyond his interview room, only their undulating rhythm - one loud voice followed by another soft, followed by both loud together, then one soft alone. Each exchange ended with some percussion, a door slam or boots marching off resolutely somewhere. He could catch no mention of his name nor any other clue that might signify some discussion of, or decision about, his case.

Yet, throughout all this, he had not been at all tempted to step outside the interview room and investigate for himself what was happening. An apathy, a listlessness was overtaking Gerry now. He was in bare, clean, warm surroundings, appetites had been satisfied, and apart from a slight bladder pressure he was perfectly comfortable. Nothing could have been further from his mind than to break the injunction laid upon him to stay where he was. He wondered idly whether a modern prison – an open prison? for light offenders? - offered such clean and pleasant living. If so, it would unquestionably be a much healthier and more civilized environment in which to spend the rest of his days than the house in Notting Hill. Very preferable. Everything found. Everything considered.

The social security. The police. The hospitals. The prisons . . .

As if to cut short such defeatist fantasy before it took too firm a hold, there was at last another knock at the door. It was the bearded policeman again. He looked different. The bollockings had taken their toll. He had been stripped of his shiny peaked driver's cap - perhaps it had been knocked off! - and he looked older than before. His overgrown and straggling eyebrows were now exposed to full view, and it was noticeable that his hair was receding. It stopped in a sad, damp fringe high above his sloping forehead. The top buttons of his tunic were undone. He did not come fully into the room but leant there in the doorway like a drunk, his hand still on the door handle. "I have come to make you an apology, sir," he said. He blinked and looked at the floor, then back at Gerry. "Will you please accept my apology, sir?"

"My dear fellow," said Gerry graciously, "you have nothing to apologize to me about. Not to me. Your treatment of me has been exemplary in every regard. You are a credit to your force, and I shall not hesitate to pass that sentiment on to your superior officers. My dear boy, you owe me no apology. Please."

"Oh, I do, sir. I do. But thank you for your kind words.

Many thanks."

He retreated, but was in such a state of confusion and distraction that before closing the door he pushed his head in a final time.

"Thank you, sir," he said once more, nodding. He looked furtively over his shoulder down the corridor, then quickly closed the door again. Gerry heard his steps retreating. He looked at his watch and sighed. He was about to get up and wander about the room to break up the monotony, when there was a second knock on the door – an impatient, resentful rap which he seemed to recognize. For a moment he thought the time had come when Anna was to be re-introduced to him, but when the door opened there was the colossus of Detective Sergeant Aldwich again, and though he could have obscured the figure of Anna Delaporte behind him, it was plain that he was on his own. The novelty of his freakishness had worn off and Gerry felt bored and oppressed by the man's return. His bulk, his ego, seemed somehow obstructive to any progress.

Again Detective Sergeant Aldwich closed the door behind him, turned about and came over to the table. He sat down opposite Gerry once more. There was no tucking up of his trousers this time, though, and his eyes were tighter now, reflecting a tension between the powerful anger he had given vent to outside, the pleasures of which he had not entirely recovered from, and the sympathy he felt obliged to summon for this meeting.

"There's been a mix-up," he said to Gerry. "And we are all very sorry." He found it necessary now to raise a hand and dig his thumb and forefinger into the corners of his eyes. He screwed up his eyes as if in some discomfort, then spoke from this position, with eyes fast shut.

"I have to start again sir, I'm afraid."

There was a pause. At last he opened his eyes. He offered a grim but sympathetic smile.

"As I said before, this is one of my most unpleasant duties, if not the most unpleasant. Tenpence - "

"Forget Tenpence!" Gerry broke in. "Forget D.S.Tenmere, officer. Please. Just give me the news."

Aldwich looked steadily at Gerry's forehead. He had arrived at the moment from which there could be no flinching.

"The news is very bad, sir. Very, very bad."

Gerry could think of nothing new to say. "What on earth has happened, officer?"

"It's really very bad, sir."

"But what has happened?"

"It concerns your wife, sir."

"But what has happened to my wife?"

There was a pause. Detective Sergeant Aldwich drew in a breath.

"She has taken her own life, sir."

Of all the eventualities which could have presented themselves at this moment, this one, which he immediately saw was quite as likely as any of the others, this one had not even crossed Gerry's mind. He felt shock, bewilderment. Could it be so? The very thought of such a thing, of her suicide, by a macabre irony, suddenly made Anna real again - a person of flesh and blood. Not the harridan of the police identikit, nor the ghastly shade of his overwrought and vindictive imagination. Then at exactly the moment she was restored to flesh and blood, she was taken away, she was finally gone. Gerry found himself overwhelmed with feeling, with an unutterable pity for this poor, long-suffering woman, who had seen her one chance in life, her one gamble for capital, for freedom, and who had seized that chance, taken her gamble, and within half a year had felt every hope turn to sand. All the terrible things he had thought about her over the last months began to jangle in his mind. What an unbelievably selfish man he had been. And not just over these last months, but always, always. What terminal grief and distress he must have caused her, and with what stoicism had she borne it all, till the last. And then to end her life, like this, in such terrible isolation, deserted, betrayed - what an infinite sadness this was.

The Detective Sergeant had already started speaking again.

"She knew we were closing in, you see, sir. She must have known there was no way out. The game was up."

Even in this moment of intense personal loss the Detective Sergeant could not refrain from taking some petty credit.

"Would you leave me alone for a few minutes, please?"

"Of course, sir."

Chapter Fourteen

No Friendly Drop

It came to light in the resumed briefing with Detective Sergeant Aldwich that the discovery of Anna Delaporte's suicide had only been made minutes before Gerry's arrival at Bangor Police Station. The news had been confidential to Aldwich at that stage, at his own discretion. The officers collecting Gerry had returned just seconds before those collecting the suspect, causing confusion for the Desk Sergeant, who, on hearing of Anna's suicide from the second group, had played safe and cancelled when there was no need, Aldwich already being 'fully apprised'. He'd jumped the gun, Aldwich explained. "Not untypical, I'm afraid," he added. "Bad timing, crossed wires, and we are all very sorry." On Aldwich's personal instructions forensic examinations had been suspended so that the bereaved might visit the cottage and identify the body immediately.

When Gerry came out of the police station, accompanied by the bearded constable, the Volvo was already full. Aldwich was in the front passenger seat and in the back were two other policemen Gerry had not met before, together with the Desk Sergeant. Why the Desk Sergeant or any of these other back-seat officers should abandon their duties for this visit was not made clear. They sat grim faced and rather squashed behind the steamy windows of the Volvo, which was sagging and very overladen. Gerry's bearded constable had his hat back on now and was altogether re-composed. He escorted Gerry briskly to the rear of the building, where they approached the only vehicle in sight, an ageing Vauxhall Chevan. On opening the passenger door Gerry noted a sharp stink of dog: this was a dog transport vehicle, a mobile kennel. Behind his passenger seat a fence of rusty netting sealed off the rear compartment. Yet, Gerry observed, his seat was covered with dog hairs. Some favourite animal was obviously allowed to ride shotgun in the front here. Some Rover, Trigger or Bess, customarily took the seat he was about to take. But he was on his way to identify the body of his wife, for goodness' sake . . . Gerry hesitated, thinking of the overcrowded Volvo, but was in no mood to make a fuss of any kind.

The Chevan rounded the building, the Volvo pulled away, and they drove in convoy back down the hill of pre-war semis into the warren of ancient, narrow streets of Bangor town centre. Gerry stared absently at this unfamiliar place, at its shops, its shoppers in their bulbous anoraks going about the streets under grey skies, buying their wares, getting on with their lives. From all this he was now removed. Over the last four months, bit by bit, day by day, he had receded, he had established distance, detachment. But only now was his alienation complete. Anna's suicide had raised a distinction between his existence and that of his fellow creatures here, by ushering in a very obvious and unnerving question. If her life had not been worth living, how could his possibly be?

The convoy took a new road through a bleak, windswept and apparently abandoned industrial estate, shabbily sign-boarded 'Bangor Business Park'. From there they picked up the A487 to Caernarfon. Gerry stared indifferently from the Chevan window at the passing countryside. The green hills were dark under leaden skies, and the sheep were just blurred, dirty tufts littered all over the place. There was an air of neglect about the landscape. No human form could he seen strolling across the hills keeping an eye on things. Walls had fallen into disrepair and some animals stood nibbling at the roadside, at risk from the traffic. Anna would have hated all of this. Why on earth had she come here, of all places?

The convoy was in no particular hurry. They took a long way round Caernarfon, leaving the castle on the right, faint in the dull afternoon, and joined the A499 coast road. The sea came into view at Pontlyfni. Gerry glanced once or twice at the beautiful, misty view of Caernarfon Bay, but he felt self-conscious looking across the constable's field of vision. He did not want to appear the sightseer on this funereal expedition. At Trevor they turned left across the Lleyn Peninsular and in another ten minutes or so they were on the outskirts of Pwllheli.

Gerry leant forward. His heart beat a little faster. He tried to discipline his thoughts, marshal his disparate feelings of guilt, grief, pity and relief.

It turned out, however, that Pwllheli itself was not their destination but rather an outreach of the town further along the coast. Towards Penrhos, the bearded constable explained. They remained on the A499 for a couple of miles beyond Pwllheli and then, after some ribbon development of drab municipal housing, the convoy took a left turn and descended seawards on an unmarked road, which eventually narrowed to a single lane. The remote, tortuous route made Gerry think again of his wife's determination to be rid of him at all costs, to be hidden from him without trace. And then - the pity of it, the pity of it! - in this terrible isolation, to be rid of both him and the whole wide world. This poignant reflection was interrupted as the Volvo slowed ahead and indicated another left turn. The bearded constable went down through the noisy gears of the Chevan and followed the Volvo onto a dirt track which, after fifty yards or so, degenerated into a lumpy path of grass and stone.

The vehicles stopped. They had arrived. The journey had taken just under thirty minutes. Winter dusk was now upon them.

On the right was a modest but well maintained bungalow. Its walls were freshly pebbledashed and its vast front window was expensively double-glazed in a white PVC frame. This polished window had the look of something for which its owners would be indebted for years to come. As well as providing the perfect spying point for the 'busybody' landlady D.S.Tenmere had mentioned - no doubt its primary purpose - it also afforded magnificent views of the sea below. Down the slope to the left was what Gerry assumed to be the original cottage, the holiday let, a tiny, blind, stony block, wedged awkwardly in a crook of the cliffs.

Another police vehicle, a personnel van, was already at the scene. Some hatless uniformed men were drinking coffee and eating sandwiches in the back. Gerry watched as Detective Sergeant Aldwich, now covered in a vast sheet of grey polythene (it had begun to drizzle) approached the van and knocked at the window. The window slid back, some remarks were exchanged, humorous to the men eating sandwiches within, and then the Detective Sergeant turned and nodded in the direction of the Chevan.

"Shall we go, then, sir?" the bearded officer asked Gerry.

Gerry said nothing but turned to his door, found the handle and pulled it back. The wet air outside was blustery and cold but refreshing after the stink of Alsatian in the Chevan. Only Detective Sergeant Aldwich and the bearded officer accompanied Gerry to the cottage. The three policemen in the back of the Volvo remained where they were, squeezed together in the warmth, and, glancing back a moment, Gerry noted that from somewhere a flask of tea or coffee and some sandwiches had appeared. The Volvo's back-seat officers were taking a break, like those in the personnel van. How infantile, Gerry observed, surprising himself with the thought. But that was the word that popped into his undefended mind - infantile. He lowered his head and frowned at the path of crazy paving at his feet, still in no mood to question any aspect of the proceedings.

Detective Sergeant Aldwich opened the door of the cottage on a gate latch and beckoned Gerry to enter. After Gerry, he bent low himself and twisted through the doorway, followed by the bearded constable, who shut the door very firmly behind them, not trusting the gate latch.

Silence.

They stood in a group, stooping together, though there was no need to stoop now they were inside. They were on the threshold of an open living area divided into two levels. The first level was furnished with a small Formica dining table. The sides of the table were folded down and there was a metal framed, canvas chair – a church hall chair - tucked in neatly at either end. The brown Formica was bare and wiped clean. Beyond the table, in the opposite wall, was an open fireplace. The second, lower level offered two light armchairs, pieces of upholstered garden furniture, that faced a sizeable window (a timber-framed, DIY prototype of the one in the bungalow) which overlooked a craggy descent to the sea. There was a wicker coffee table, glass-topped, immediately in front of the garden chairs, and on this could be seen a sheet of paper bearing some writing. A litre bottle of Gordon's gin served as paperweight.

It was cold inside the stony holiday let. The black remains of a feeble fire lay in the grate.

Visible at the top of the left hand chair was a head of quite tightly curled, dyed auburn hair. The hair was just a shade darker than Anna's, or rather the very shade she had when she returned from the hairdressers'. Two thin but still shapely legs were also visible, protruding beneath the coffee table, their feet in polished, black leather shoes, footwear of the kind invariably labelled 'classic'. The sight quickened a sudden compassion and tenderness in Gerry. That Anna's life, and his life, their lives together, should end like this after more than thirty years. Thirty years. That those legs and feet should have carried her here, faithfully, finally, to this place, to that upholstered garden chair, and then stopped, come to rest, and the blood stopped within them, cooled within them, when her heart stopped, and her life was at last sloughed off, over and done with.

And following those gentler feelings a wave of guilt. All of this, all of it, was a consequence of his utterly selfish actions.

"Shall we go down?" said Detective Sergeant Aldwich.

His voice was theatrically deep and soft, fulsome in its professional tact.

The group moved away from the door, each man straightening as he did so. Gerry followed the two policemen across some woven matting on the first level, past the fireplace, and down to the bare stone floor of the second level. No proper carpet of any description, anywhere. At night the place must have been freezing. That fire in the grate! That pitiful attempt at a fire in the grate! And these sparse, inferior furnishings. The garden chairs, in December. That mat, that wicker table. The mean-spiritedness of the busybody landlady imbued the room. Quite extraordinary. Evident in every aspect of her holiday let.

Gerry followed the two policemen to the chairs. When the officers stepped in front of the left chair, taking up position before the window - the oblong, warped and leaky, DIY window - Gerry did the same, falling into line at their side without hesitation.

He felt the draught from the window against the back of his legs. Gusts of the sea breeze outside made low whistles, soft and lewd, through the warped frame, into the morbid silence.

There was no look of peacefulness in the dead face. The cares of the world had not ebbed away, they had only stopped with the beat of her heart. But her hands were peaceful, folded in her lap. Her face was very pale of course, but there was the impression still that it had been pale in life also. The lips were made up with a hardly noticeable, subtly contrasting lipstick, a very light, soft pink. A heart shaped face, beautiful perhaps, thirty years ago. The mouth was open but not agape. Her front teeth were slightly protrusive. She had been a thin woman, delicate, frail. Recently she had not eaten properly, she had not taken care of herself, she had not been properly cared for, had suffered an appalling neglect. She was dressed in a blue cotton suit with a pale blue blouse beneath. She had wanted to be found presentable. Hands folded in her lap. Her classic shoes were black and shiny and uncreased and looked new, in fact, rather than polished. Bought for the occasion, perhaps. This was not a woman who had suffered a gradual descent into irretrievable degradation, this was a woman who had made a cold and rational decision earlier today, or perhaps even before coming here, a woman who had wanted to remain elegant and self-possessed to the end.

The note was brief and in a steady italic hand. Gerry could read it easily, upside down, from where he stood. It said: *I do not want any more to lead such a lonely existence.* Then, on a separate line. *It is no one's fault.*

No one's fault.

The glass from which she had been drinking was on the floor beside her chair, and next to it a large, supermarket size bottle of tonic, and the telltale brown medicine bottle, now empty. This close the scent of gin was strong as formaldehyde.

Detective Sergeant Aldwich spoke again, his voice grave, burdened with its own importance, and its fulsome sympathy.

"Mr Delaporte, is this your wife, sir?"

There was a pause, an ominous silence.

"Was this my wife, you mean." Gerry replied, without thinking. The schoolmaster's reflex. He shook his head. "No," he added. "She most definitely was not."

Detective Sergeant Aldwich stared hard at Gerry's profile. But Gerry did not turn to him. His eyes were still set on the face of the suicide victim.

"Are you sure?"

There was an accusatory note to the question, as if Gerry were now deliberately obstructing police inquiries.

"I have never been more certain of anything in my life."

Attitudes hardened towards Gerry on the journey back to the police station, but he was in a distracted state of mind and did not care. Instead of being preoccupied with his wife's evasion of detection, and all the catastrophic consequences of that defeat – from here, he suspected, police efforts would dwindle to nothing: the case had proved insoluble - Gerry was now led astray by a melancholy speculation. Why had that woman taken her own life? How could she have found herself so alone in the world? Her dead body had stirred Gerry. From tiny indications, her sense of dress, her make-up, her handwriting, the brief frankness of her note, he had deduced that she had been a well-educated and intelligent woman, and certainly, to his mind, a very prepossessing woman. So how could she have found herself so alone? His thoughts only had to travel this circuit a couple of times before he recognized the singular irony of such questions. If his body had been discovered in similar circumstances, could not the same have been thought about him? He could dress well, given the means, the adequate means, to free himself from his Harris Tweed and his beige trousers, and he had an authentic italic hand, and if his face were clean shaven and dabbed, perhaps, with some discreet, alluring after-shave, his sensitive features could have been thought to have had a boyish charm once, he was sure, even in death. Thus Gerry built up a most appealing picture of his own corpse in the garden chair next to the woman's, and he deduced from the compatibility in this picture that in life, as in death, these two people could have had much in common - but never, ever, a suicide pact. How he lamented the lost opportunity of meeting this woman, and to have missed that opportunity by just a train ride, a few hours. Had they only met, had they only had their chance, Gerry was convinced he could have said something to her which would have assured her there were indeed people of her own kind in the world, that the rest of her life could have been spent in rewarding companionship, not indefinite loneliness. She was clearly a woman of independent means. She might well have been prepared to share those means with a man of similar sensibilities, a quiet, thoughtful and deserving gentleman of modest tastes and sincere disposition. Oh Lord! - how close fortune had been to bringing them together, and in such ironic circumstances. He was looking for his false love and he might have found his true. And in a further reversal, she, like Romeo, had drunk the phial too soon, and left Gerry with Juliet's line:

> *O churl! drunk all, and left no friendly drop*
> *To help me after?*

As the Chevan drew in hard to the police compound Gerry's idle head was tossed against the door and a mawkish tear was shaken from the corner of his eye. The engine stopped, the handbrake was jerked up on its ratchet, and Gerry found himself brought to a standstill also. He had become an inert force. There seemed no conceivable reason to leave the police dog-van. Dusk had thickened. He sat there staring through the windscreen at an overgrown hawthorn bush the other side of the compound fence. Its wet branches thrashed in the wind and tore themselves against the barbed wire and the concrete corner post. Gerry stared at the bush, at its indifferent lashings and thrashings in the grey twilight, and he thought, Yes, the world could very well get along without me too. It was not an unpleasant thought.

"Come on then! We haven't got all day!"

The bearded officer's tone was abrupt. Gerry realized that he had let them all down, the whole party who had deserted their duties in order to be present at the solution of a case, and now there was ill-feeling, resentment, and he no longer had any protective significance. Most assuredly there would be no more rides in the Volvo. No more tea and biscuits. He decided it would be wise to stay exactly where he was and negotiate things from here, from the passenger seat of the dog vehicle, in the corner of the compound.

"Look," he said, still staring vacantly out of the windscreen at the hawthorn bush, "presumably I am now surplus to requirements here. Would it not be possible, constable, for you to run me down to the railway station?"

When there was no response to his request he turned to his bearded companion, who now looked at him with a mixture of amusement and astonishment. The constable cocked his hat back and his head retracted incredulously on its hairy neck.

"I can't run around giving you lifts in police vehicles!"

"Why not? You gave be a lift from the rail station, didn't you? Why not to it?"

"That was different."

"Why?"

The officer was silent a moment, at a loss.

"Look, constable, you have been jolly decent to me today. Jolly decent. I have been so impressed by your good conduct that I fully intend to commend you to your superior officers. I have already told you that." Gerry twisted round on the furry seat so that he faced the constable more comfortably. "Now then," he resumed, "I know I might not look like much just at the moment, but I am an educated man, and I can write a good letter. A damn good letter. It would go on your file. On your record. And it would heal the breach rent this afternoon by my visit. That was my fault. Entirely my fault. The upset between you and your superior officers. I should like to make amends somehow. I can do you good, constable. I can and I will. In return all I ask of you, in this life, is a five minute lift back to the railway station."

The constable took a long, deep breath. Gerry saw that his words had had some effect. He was mildly surprised.

"All right. But I'll have to pop in and clear it."

"Pop in and clear it?"

"It'll have to be cleared with the D.S."

"Look . . ." Gerry went so far as to touch the sleeve of the constable's tunic. "All I'm asking for is a five minute lift to the station. A five minute lift. Look at me." The constable, used to doing as he was told, looked at Gerry. "Look at me," Gerry repeated. "I am not a young fit man like yourself. I am an old, sick man. I am ill. Possibly very ill. Terminally ill. Let us just pop down to the station. Then I'll be gone, and you'll all be rid of me. You personally will have done everyone a favour, a bigger favour to your fellow officers than to me, perhaps. I left of my own free will, disappeared into the dusk, into the mists of the streets below, the mists of time - so case closed, file put away, back in the cabinet, and that's that. It won't take five minutes. Five minutes." Gerry held up an open hand. "Five minutes." His voice was soft but not wheedling, despite a gnawing impatience within him.

"It'll have to be cleared with the D.S. There's no way round it."

"Well, we'll speak to him on the radio on the way!"

Gerry pointed to a dangling, antique looking handset, hitched to a clip on the dashboard by its grubby flex.

The officer grunted. "Doesn't work," he said. "Any road, you must get clearance before, not during an operation."

"But this isn't an operation!" Gerry protested. "This is a lift. You don't have to clear a lift." Gerry slapped his knee and laughed dismissively. "Just a five minute lift to the station. For goodness' sake - it does credit to your initiative, man. You don't have to clear it with the D.S. He's got much more important things on his mind. Much bigger fish to fry, poor fellow. He'll thank you for doing this."

"I have to clear it." The officer opened his door wide. Gerry saw that it was no use trying to argue the point further. The officer was out the van and walking away now. Gerry leant across the gear stick and called after him:

"Well, clear it with the Desk Sergeant, then. Not that fat fellow, all right?"

He had assumed he was referring to a mutual enemy in the superior officer, the man who, less than a couple of hours ago, had given this bearded bobby such a 'bollocking', but his indelicate reference to a superior officer brought the constable's feet to a halt on the tarmac. It was as if the constable had been called to attention, right there in the yard. Gerry had made a costly misjudgement of the security, the pride and pleasure, the honour, the love, even, to be found in a certain kind of loyalty. That word popped up again. Infantile. The constable turned about and retraced his steps to the car. Gerry sat back in his own seat. "Oh hell," he muttered to himself, knowing that this was the end.

The constable came round to his side, stooped and looked through the window.

"What did you say?"

"I merely said - "

"I heard exactly what you said! Now get out of that police vehicle!"

Gerry opened the passenger door and the constable pulled it wide. With some difficulty, using both arms on the door frame, Gerry drew himself out of the Chevan. He was unsteady on his legs. His fever had burned him out. The biscuits, even the sugary bourbons, had been used up long ago.

Chapter Fifteen

The Order Book

Gerry arrived back at Euston on the milk train at a little after two in the morning. He had no money at all, having squandered everything on sandwiches, coffee and chocolate when he changed trains at Birmingham New Street. He had not even kept the fare for a night-bus down the Euston Road. Some dreadful recklessness had overcome him at Birmingham New Street. Coffee in hand, he had pumped his last few coins into an antique chocolate machine on the platform.

On leaving the shelter of Euston station it was salutary to remember how, in his past life, he had perceived lone, early morning stragglers such as himself, as they made their way aimlessly along London's streets. Returning with Anna in the car after some concert or other he could never pass one by without remark. "Now, just look at that poor chap," he'd mutter. "How ever does he keep himself going, poor fellow?" Anna said nothing. She looked away. In the incredulous, half-amazed tone in which Gerry made such remarks, he implied that he himself could never sink so low, because he would find life at that level quite intolerable, not worth living. Which was actually a strange way of feeling sorry for himself rather than the figure outside. My life is grim enough, he implied, and I couldn't endure any additional unhappiness. I should get rid of myself in some way rather than fall to that. "How people cling to life . . ." was another aside in similar vein, which Anna met with either more stony silence, or an impatient sigh. He remembered stopping once, in the wee small hours, to allow an ancient figure, dressed in a coat over his pyjamas, stooped over a walking frame, to shuffle across a pedestrian crossing. Some asylum or hospital escapee. The man was in his carpet slippers. It was bitterly cold and wet. Gerry had sat there, attentive to the man's creeping progress, the wipers on, the car heater turned up full, while Anna patted her handbag in the passenger seat. She knew very well that he could have crossed without stopping for the invalid at all. The man raised a pale hand, whether in thanks to Gerry or to defend himself from the headlights, it was impossible to tell. But what was it, Gerry had thought, that burned within this man still? Forgetting himself for once, Gerry had seen something admirable in this invalid's tenacity.

Ah, but now, carless, making his own weary way down the vast and hostile Euston Road, the taxis swishing by, he realized that of course there was no strength in such tenacity, no more strength in it than in that fellow's grip on his walking frame. That way of looking at things was just the romanticism of one who sat comfortably in a warm car, listening to the radio, or to the hum of the fan heater. No.

People clung to a lonely and impoverished existence only through weakness and fear, which is what made suicide courageous and ennobling now, as exemplified by the woman he had seen yesterday. That woman. Her gin bottle. Her clear italic hand. She had done it.

But her way was not for Gerry. He shook his head and trembled even to contemplate it. He was spineless and contemptible, yes, but there was another reason which precluded that course of action. He could not bear, not for an instant, to imagine that his wife might be his beneficiary, the sole executor of his estate. If he died intestate she stood to collect from all manner of policies he could not even calculate from here. There was life assurance still outstanding, endowments, tax-exempt savings schemes, multifoliate policies about to burgeon into magnificent bloom in the next fifteen months or so, coinciding with his sixtieth birthday or thereabouts. He would deny her those at any cost. She would not visit his corpse in some anonymous London morgue. No. Never. She would not read his brief and elegant suicide note, written in his own italic hand, taken from beneath the spring of D.S.Tenmere's (old Tenpence's) clipboard - *There's a lot of circumstantial, madam* – and passed across the clean Formica table, the table with the hardwood edging, passed across to her – *The news is very bad, Mrs Delaporte. Very, very bad. It concerns your husband, madam* - Oh no. No no no. That was not going to happen.

Once more then, having set out confident that he should never be returning to dear old Claremont Villas, he made his return. But after such a day, and after the wearing walk from the station, Gerry's spirit was numb to any sense of defeat. He picked his way up the stairs by the light of the forty watt bulb he had bought for the first floor landing, a recent replacement. Funny, wasn't it, how no one else had bothered to replace that bulb, to make everyone's life just that little bit easier. Oh no, they all depended on Gerry's bulb. Of course they did. And when that blew they would wait until he bought another. Hah! *Two Strong Arms,* indeed. Two limp wrists, more like. Two lazy shits, more like. What a pair of fucking parasites!

Gerry stopped on his landing. There were sounds from up there. Muffled sounds. Not their sounds. He struggled a moment to recognize them, or rather to meet his understanding of the sounds head-on. The slow smack, and then the low groan of pleasure. They were at it again. Webb, and the tiny Jake fellow, presumably. Getting on with their unspeakable business. What had Jake done this time? Bad, bad boy. But perhaps it wasn't Jake but some other cooperative slave. Gerry shook his feeble fist and shouted up the stairs:

"Fuck you! . . . Fuck you one and all!"

Oh dear, oh dear.

What profane wretch am I?

The sounds stopped and he heard the door open upstairs, the Office door, presumably. Unless Mik and Kim . . . *Justice must be seen to be done! . . . Pour encourager les autres! . . .* He shook his head. All too much. All too much to contemplate. He unlocked the bedroom he had never meant to unlock again, collapsed on the mattress he had hoped never to lie down on again, and, as furtive steps descended outside, he fell into a restless, fitful sleep.

He woke after just a few hours, too early for the sleep to have done any good. His mind was racing and his body feverish. He could concentrate on nothing for more than a few seconds. There was some unidentified anxiety running ahead of his concentration, and all he could do was chase it round and round with a few lean and mangy speculations.

At last the contest for survival itself had begun.

He had woken from a dream in which he relived the interview with the faceless young man in the social security office, the man who had told him that the payment for his second class ticket to Bangor and back "would be deducted from his benefit". Given that the benefit was paid fortnightly this meant that the visit to north Wales had wiped out his income for the next two weeks. Of course the Department of Health & Social Security was waiting to hear some favourable news about a change in the circumstances of Mr Gerald Delaporte Esquire, who had been on their books for more than four months now. But he could offer no such news. In which event, how did he stand? Surely they must see that his expedition to Pwllheli had been undertaken in good faith? He had not been popping off to "some holiday resort in Wales". The police had led him to believe they had solved his case. He had listened to the assurances from the C.I.D, from two Detective Sergeants, no less. Messrs. Tenmere and Aldwich. Tenpence and Aldy. The fact that they had turned out to be a pair of incompetents, a couple of buffoons, clowns, oafs, was surely neither here nor there. Insubmissible evidence, m'lud. Surely anyone would have done as he did.

Yet, yet, yet - he knew only too well that it need not appear so straightforward to those the other side of the cubicle glass, to the obese young woman with blue oval glasses, or the sour Scot with dyed black hair, whom he had taken such pains to avoid, and who now, no doubt, would be specifically assigned to his claim -

Ah, gewd afterrnewn, sirr. Little Lorrd Fontlerroy, ay prresume, sirr . . .

And even if he did persuade her to act in his favour it would take a week at least, and many irksome visits to the offices, to get an adjusted payment through. So how was he to feed himself for the next few days, or the next two weeks? How was he to live? Was he expected just to starve away and die?

This anxiety was the hare on the track, and behind it sped a ragbag bunch of desperate solutions.

In lane one: *Scrounger.*

Should he approach Mik and Kim for a loan? Or if not a loan, which did seem a little pointless, could he not ask if he might share their food and their tea for the next fortnight, or until he was in receipt of an emergency payment from the social security? He would join them upstairs at appointed times of the day for his meals. What an appalling prospect!

In lane two: *Try Again.*

Should he approach Alec Webb – *Sir* Alec Webb! - for a loan? But Webb had already made clear his position on this matter and it seemed unlikely he would reverse it.

In lane three: *Tea leaf.*

Should he attempt to rob Alec Webb? While Webb was attending to life and love at Claremont Villas and administering his various blessings, Gerry could make a swift return to Observatory Gdns. The Thai girl could be fed some harmless lie about an errand he was running for Webb, something about the diocesan newsletter perhaps, then once inside the Webb residence he need only take some minor item, some jade or marble figurine, the brass tray from Calcutta . . .

Good form. Lots of promise. But not the favourite.

In lane four: *Scam.*

This last hound came up from the rear and edged by the tiring pack. It nodded knowingly to him, its wet tongue lolling and its foul breath coming fast as it closed on the finishing line. Should he work? What he had in mind was not exactly gainful employment, which he would not get in any case, he knew well enough. If he tramped the streets from dawn to dusk, and ill as he was and with no food to sustain him he was in no fit state to do that anyway, but even if he staggered from kitchen to kitchen looking for scraps and some washing up, he would always be the third or fourth in line, after all those young fellows from the hostel. And good luck to them. No. Gerry had something more artful up his sleeve.

Two Strong Arms was now fully installed on the second floor. Gerry had heard the telephone ring once or twice. Mik and Kim answered it in shifts, a major advance on the rota system. Webb had evidently had his own motives for inviting the couple to move in here. Gerry also knew from his regular snoopings around upstairs that two shabby bags of tools, each with its mark of collective ownership – T.S.A., identified in strips of yellow insulation tape - were kept tucked behind the door of the office. These were cooperatively owned tools or stand-by kits of some description. Gerry did not intend to accomplish a job of work for the Cooperative: what he had in mind was more a crude swindle. Using his voice and bourgeois charm to best effect he would make an appointment on the telephone to view a prospective job. He'd take any job at all from the famous order book, anything at all. He'd not be fussy like young Mr Fitzroy. And when he arrived at the client's house, his bag of tools in hand, he would look the job over, make all the right noises, and offer a quite unturndownable quote. His quote accepted, he would ask for a very reasonable advance for his working materials. After taking the money he'd pop out to buy the said materials - casually leaving his tools behind, to lend confidence - and then he'd simply renege on the deal. Never come back. Pocket the cash. The inspiration for the idea came from his own experience. He himself had been suckered by builders - twice! - in similar fashion. (The second time the builder had been an old boy from his school. A dull, quiet lad, whom he had thought, until the swindle, that he had got along with rather well.)

Gerry sighed and turned over on his damp mattress. He had been too exhausted when he came in to hook up his curtains and his room had filled with the grey light of a December morning. He had not undressed last night, except to take off his shoes. But shoes were not needed for the first part of his plan, so no further preparation was required. He just had to sit up, stand up, and hustle his limp body to the door. Once outside he must act quickly and in stealth. There was no time to waste in washing himself or making himself in any way more presentable. He needed no mirror to know how he looked - ashen-faced, grey-stubbled, sunken-eyed . . .

He slipped out of his room in his socks and went straight upstairs, keeping to the walls and the edges of the boards. He knew well the more treacherous ones. All the hours spent squatting about in the dark listening to Mik and Kim now paid an unexpected dividend.

The first obstacle was the Office door itself. A couple of days ago, when Gerry had been up here last, it had been bare, handleless and unsecured. Things like locks offended the free-thinking ethos of Two Strong Arms. But in his absence some new realism had taken hold. The Office door now bore the mark of ownership, the name *Two Strong Arms* was signpainted in red paint - Kim's handiwork, presumably - and the word OFFICE was printed in black stencil beneath it; and just as fresh were the shiny brass padlock and chain securing the door through a chrome handle, a cupboard door-handle, screwed laterally to the centre stile. Gerry muttered an oath under his breath. The hasp on the jamb looked weak and inferior though, some nonsense from the corner shop rather than a proper ironmongers'. He returned to his rooms for his pliers and a screwdriver. With only the mildest persuasion the hasp separated from its mounting. He pushed the door open at first gently, then swiftly, silencing the whining hinge.

He first looked behind the door. There was little point in pursuing matters if there were no tools to guarantee his plan. Both bags were there, though. And beyond them, incongruously and yet so appropriately, squashed into the very corner behind the door, was a pair of carpet slippers. Webb's and Jake's, of course. Owned cooperatively. Cheap slippers of a tartan design. Gerry didn't hesitate. He took them and put them on. His feet were numb and they were a perfect fit.

Oh, Cinderella!

He returned to the bags, wondering for a moment if it were worth simply stealing the tools and selling them. He bent down and inspected the contents. No. The tools were secondhand, battered, worn and blunt, they wouldn't fetch anything, not even on the Portobello Road, not even as bookends or artefacts for a bourgeois mantelpiece . . . What about the telephone? But the telephone was a scratched and shabby instrument imported from the old Office. Rubbish. Worthless.

The Chesterfield sat squarely under the window, an absurd, incongruous thing. Gerry sat down on it for a moment, crossed his slippered feet and shut his eyes. The leather was hard, cold and unyielding. Should he not just wait here on the Chesterfield to be found, and then, when found here, in the grey and chilly gloom, sitting on the sofa, in his tartan slippers, after his aborted break-in, when found here on the Chesterfield, should he not just trust to human charity - wait for the warm and gentle embrace of the brotherhood and sisterhood of Two Strong Arms?

He opened his eyes. Across the room, leaning against the wall, were Kim's still lifes, as yet unhung. Oils, no less. One was just some boring lumps of fruit – bananas or mangoes - difficult to tell, rotting in a wooden bowl. The bowl itself seemed almost vertical, about to tip its lumps out the canvas. No perspective, Kim, you see. No perspective still on life. That's your problem. The second canvas was a bold attempt at a blue Chinese vase, with a single, gaudy yellow flower – a sunflower, of course - sticking out the top on a crooked stem. The dragon on the vase wound in limp and straggling fashion, mostly tail, no clear delineation of the head or limbs at all . . . Well, awfully sorry and all that, but it's complete rubbish, Kim, I'm afraid. Absolute, worthless rubbish. Gerry stood and crossed to the paintings, hands in pockets. In the tartan slippers his feet were still numb. He set one solid, tartan foot against Kim's fruit bowl and pushed. Pushed harder. The masterpiece dented, then tore. He did the same to her Chinese vase, which ripped instantly, dramatically, right across, from one corner to the other. From arse to tit, if it had been a nude.

Oh, if only it had been a nude! A self-portrait.

He stood back and glanced about the Office again.

Come on! *Get on with it.*

He eased himself behind Webb's desk, pulled out the kitchen chair and sat down. He noticed, to his consternation, that the desk was a schoolteacher's desk, not dissimilar to the one he had had in his classroom in Ipswich. This was just the kind of association to which he was vulnerable right now. It paralyzed him. Here he was, back behind his desk, the pillory behind which he'd been mocked for thirty years. He sat there with his eyes shut and breathed in deeply for a whole minute, trying to regain composure under a deluge of shouts, of screams, of slapping rulers, stamping feet, banging desks – *Delashit! Delatit! Delaprick!* - but he was too abject now to defend himself against himself. He opened his eyes, ran his tongue over his stubbly, feverish upper lip, and tried to pull the drawer. It came out a fraction only, then jammed. Gerry bent down and peered in. The drawer had snagged on the cover of a large book.

The order book.

He fingered the cover down, released the drawer and pulled it open.

What a hefty volume. He had to use both hands to prise it from its drawer. He held it up to the grey light and blew some dust off its cover. It struck him as the kind of tome from which dust should be blown. He ran his hands over the cover. It was a handsome marbled scarlet, and the thick binding of the book was of a rich violet hue. Good heavens, this was more the kind of thing one might have found in Observatory Gdns. seventy years ago, tucked in the kitchen dresser for household accounts, and made ready for monthly inspection to the head of an Edwardian household. It was magnificent!

Gerry settled himself at the desk, determined to do this justice.

He stroked the cover of the book reverently, then lifted it from the top right corner, as if it were a bible on a pulpit.

After the fly leaves, of which there were several of various thicknesses, the first double page inside was ruled into no less than thirteen columns. Each column was headed in an immaculate black copperplate script: *Caller's Name & Address/ Caller's Tel. Number/ Job Description/ Worker Required/ Worker Assigned/ Switchboard Worker/*

Date Call Received/ Date Job Begun/ Date Job Completed/ Date Payment Received/ Other Comments/ Tax paid at 7% to Two Strong Arms A/c./Date tax paid.

At the foot of the page was a further inscription: *I certify the statements above to be authentic and correct, Signed .... Manager.*

Though the length of the page offered space for fifty entries at least, only half a dozen or so had been made. Yet the page had been signed and closed at the bottom by A.J. Webb, for it was his egotistical signature next to the title *Manager.*

Well, well, well. This was quite a find. Gerry nodded in amused disbelief. Such rigour. How grand this was, truly grand. The Manager, indeed.

The same man, doing the same job . . .

Regrettably there was little evidence that the standard of presentation set by the Manager at the head of the columns was emulated by the workers in his employ, when they got around to filling in their bits. Only Kim, predictably enough, whose name appeared twice in the *Switchboard Worker* column, had made any effort to keep the page tidy. There were columns left blank. There were entries crossed out or reversed from column to column. Dates were entered in impossible sequences. No tax whatever had been paid. Not a penny. Worst of all, on the second job, which had been for the fly-posting of five hundred publicity posters for a new sports wear shop called *Sportif,* there was an obscenity in the *Other Comments* column. It read simply: *This job nearly fucking killed me! Never again!* Alec Webb had put a line through this *Other Comment* in his black ink, initialled the deletion, *A.J.W.,* and added sternly – *Keep it clean, Jake. See me, please.*

Gerry sighed and turned the page. Again the columns were set out, but as yet there had been no entries. He turned back and examined the dates of the last call. It had been made a week ago. Nothing had come in since then. This had been another fly-posting assignment, again for *Sportif,* but as yet no Worker had been assigned to it. *Nearly fucking killed me! Never again!* . . . Gerry looked back at the first assignment entered in the book which dated from early March. No worker had taken this one up either. What lazy animals! What lazy shits! Webb would have done better to send out his primary school miscreants! Gerry bent close and studied the entry. The call had come from a Mrs Jones in Hampstead Garden Suburb, and under the Job Description was written simply, *Cat-flap*. How much could one charge for the fitting of a cat-flap? That of course depended very much upon the client, and Hampstead Garden Suburb was not at all a bad address. There was just the possibility this would be worth checking out. He tore the page from the ledger, folded it and put it away in his pocket.

Chapter Sixteen

Mrs Jones

Hampstead Garden Suburb, like so much of suburban London, is a deceptive place, but its deceptiveness adds no intrigue. The nest of streets and closes it comprises is surrounded by attractive features. Both Hampstead Golf Course and Highgate Golf Course are virtually within a stone's throw. Hampstead Heath itself is not far, and there are the more modest but still pleasant Lyttleton Playing fields nearby. But Hampstead Garden Suburb actually begins on a short stretch of the dreary A1 called 'Market Place'. All main routes north are filtered through zones such as 'Market Place': strings of traffic lights and small-time shops which clot the six lane thoroughfares. An angular and unsightly elevated walkway, low against the grey sky, is the first sign of such a zone. The road is uncrossable by any other means. The railings of the walkway have stained its concrete flanks sore with rust, and streamers of bright litter are trapped all along its span. Without the support of the colourful walkway, the grey shroud hanging over the shops and flats would fall to earth and cover Market Place forever. The architecture is Bauhaus: curved, metal casement windows, rusted and warped, and doorless entrances between shop fronts, ugly holes offering access to cars, cats, dogs and tenants. No amount of heat from whatever source will ever warm the rooms of these leaky buildings. It will always be drawn away in the slipstream of the lorries and cars hurrying by to vistas new.

Gerry alighted at the bus stop here with his Two Strong Arms tool bag at his side. He stood on the pavement, finding his bearings, in his carpet slippers. After the hard miles in his brogues the day before, on Bangor's granite, on the concrete platforms of Birmingham New Street, and on the long empty pavements of Euston Road at 2 am., their comfort was a small delight.

Mrs Jones had sounded educated, refined even, though her voice had a worrying, neurotic shrillness. Gerry had built some hopes firstly upon the address, and then upon this shaky voice. These hopes were not quite dashed as he looked about Market Place, not until he discovered that Mrs Jones' address was above a greengrocer's shop. She had said she lived, "above a florist's". The greengrocer sold a few bunches of flowers from a couple of pails on the pavement. Mrs Jones' trite and clichéd, petit bourgeois pretensions about her address blew away the last wisps of confidence.

Yet he was here, he had arrived, and succeed he must, for he had spent the few pence Kim had given him to buy some milk on the telephone call and his bus fare, and he was again without adequate means of any description.

Before setting out, he'd popped upstairs and offered to get his housemates anything they needed from the corner shop. An unprecedented act of selflessness on his part that provoked no suspicion, laziness being the better part of trust where Mik and Kim were concerned. Kim had come to the door in her nightdress, her purse already open, smiling dopily, her nipples bristling in the cold through her thin nightdress. All at once Gerry had been within reaching distance.

Lying to her had been a pleasure.

He ventured within the hole at the side of the greengrocer's shop and found a concrete stairway on the right which led to the flats above. With each step he took an unpleasant feline smell grew stronger, until he reached the dark corridor above, which gave access to the front doors of the flats. Here the smell balled itself into such a stench he was all but forced back down the stairs. He could breathe only through his mouth, and in doing so he coated his tongue with a taste that brought to mind what a cat did with its own tongue. Mrs Jones' door was opposite the stairwell. Gerry noted with some apprehension the fierce scratch marks reaching up to the keyhole.

He put down his tool bag, which weighed so heavily on body and spirit, and knocked.

A short, portly woman of about fifty opened the door. Her hair, dark and long, was scraped back and clasped, exposing a haggard face. She had a small knife in her hand, a fruit knife. It was smeared with what looked like chocolate. Her eyes, of the same dull brown as the chocolate, darted this way and that over Gerry's face, his person, his tool bag, his tartan slippers.

"Yes?"

The refined voice.

Just above the florist's. You'll see.

"Mrs Jones?"

"The same."

"Good morning to you, Mrs Jones." Gerry left space for a return salutation, but there was none. He pressed on. "I'm Gerry Delaporte from Two Strong Arms. I have come to fix your cat-flap."

Gerry smiled.

Mrs Jones pressed her wrist to her forehead and the chocolated knife pointed up across her brow. A sharp and newish knife. She shut her eyes in pained exasperation, whether with Gerry or her failing memory it was difficult to tell. "Oh, I'm sorry. Yes, of course. I'd expected someone younger. I'm sorry. Do come in."

"I rang earlier," said Gerry meaninglessly, to cover the slight about his age. He picked up his tool bag and stepped past Mrs Jones into her flat. To his disbelief he found that the stench of cats was even stronger indoors. It was something quite noxious. He felt faint, unable to breathe it in.

"Fit a cat-flap," said Mrs Jones, closing the door behind them, sealing out the cold but precious draught.

He could not speak, could not breathe.

"Hmmn?"

"What's the matter? Cat got your tongue? Ha! . . . I said fit a cat-flap. Not fix one."

Gerry smiled and nodded.

Without inviting him further into her home, Mrs Jones stepped past Gerry, hesitating a moment to scowl at his tool bag, at its *T. S. A.* in yellow insulation tape, letting it be known that both the tool bag and Gerry himself fell a long way short of her expectations. She walked on with head held high to her kitchenette at the end of the hallway. Oh, today she had a tradesman in, you see. A workman. Terrible nuisance. What a bore.

She resumed what she must have been doing in the kitchenette when Gerry had knocked, which was carefully slicing up a Mars Bar on a side plate with the new fruit knife. Gerry watched her cutting up the chocolate bar, watched the knife, listened to the sharp click of steel on china.

"I hope you haven't brought one with you."

"Hmmn?"

She glanced up at Gerry and spoke to him more loudly, sternly, as if he were hard of hearing. "I say, I hope you have not brought one with you! A cat-flap!"

Gerry shook his head emphatically. He felt increasingly self-conscious with the Two Strong Arms bag in his hand. Perhaps this pretence was beyond him after all. Perhaps he should just drop the bag and run away, like a boy scared of being found out. But where to?

"Because I've already got one," continued Mrs Jones, and she sucked her fingers and looked up from her work with the Mars Bar. She stared hard at Gerry, as if she suspected that he had been about to try to sell her something very inferior at an inflated price.

Gerry spoke at last. Despite his best efforts, some disappointment came through.

"You've already got one."

"I've already got one!" repeated Mrs Jones with some triumph, and she reached up to a kitchen shelf and fetched down a polythene wrapper containing some shiny aluminium device. "Bought it months and months ago. Before I phoned you lot up." She approached Gerry and offered him the cat-flap. He set down his bag and took it. No sooner did he have it in his hands than some screws fell to the floor.

"Careful! For goodness' sake!" Mrs Jones' voice was shrill now and full of panic, as it had been on the telephone. "Don't lose any of those! They're more than your job's worth!"

Gerry stooped to pick up the shiny screws from the lino.

And suddenly he was sweating. He was swept away from here by another involuntary memory. He was back in his classroom, amid his tormentors, last lesson of the afternoon. He was scrabbling about the floor for a piece of chalk. But the floors at school had smelt of disinfectant, of chemical lemons and limes, because they were cleaned daily, thoroughly, by the ancillary staff. The cleaners. The workers. People of the working class. Cleaners who came in at three-thirty sharp at the end of the teaching day, when he was packing up and about to go home, came in with their cloths and buckets and Squeezy sponges -

"Good afternoon, Mr Delaporte."

Oh, the shame of it! He had taught some of their children. Taught them nothing at all, nothing whatever - un, deux, trois, rien! - and then their mothers or fathers came in to clean his room for him, with their cloths and buckets and Squeezy sponges, at the end of the working day.

"Good afternoon, Mr Delaporte. Have you had a busy day?"

And all the time they knew, of course, they knew, from what their children said, and then they put it in their own terms -

Washout. Failure. Duffer. Dud.

Gerry hadn't thought he was still capable of feeling anything like this, anything so hot, so molten as this shame, which overcame him as he scrabbled around for the cat-flap screws. But it was still there, fresh as the day he had retired, all the burning guilt and disgrace he'd kept in check for thirty years, it was still all there, undiminished, ready to erupt with the first backward glance. His exile, his days in the wilderness, his sacrifice, his forty days and forty nights, had expunged nothing, achieved absolutely nothing. There could be no reconciliation. The feelings could never be expunged, exchanged, exhausted.

But here was Mrs Jones' linoleum floor, and Mrs Jones' floor was sticky with cat urine and what smelt like - but could it really be? - cat semen? An ammoniacal scent. Where were the animals that befouled this place? Where were the culprits?

Right! Own up! Who did it? It'll be easier on all of you in the long run!

Gerry stood with the rescued screws.

"So where are your cats, Mrs Jones?"

"Oh, I never see them by day. Then at night they come howling and scratching at the door there. You've never heard anything like it!"

Gerry decided that he was not within a human household at all, rather he had stepped inside a pets' toilet. Mrs Jones was one of those dismally English people who, having failed to relate to the rest of their species, turn to the animal kingdom instead. But her chosen creatures had not taken to her, they would not suck, they preferred the wilds of Hampstead Heath or Lyttleton Playing fields, and now things had come to such a pass that they used her home simply as a convenience, as somewhere to sleep off the day's excesses, to excrete and copulate in the dry.

Mrs Jones returned to her kitchenette and picked up the plate of sliced Mars Bar. She took a fork from the draining rack and then stood there in the doorway of the kitchenette and began to eat her Mars Bar, slice by delicious slice.

Chewing steadily, she said, "What's your quote, then, Mr Delaporte?"

From the moment she had opened the door she had sustained this curt, defensive manner, wary of any chicanery, trying to keep one step ahead. Ironically, Gerry felt offended by this. He knew himself to be an honest and trustworthy man, in this simple sense, but of course on this occasion Mrs Jones was absolutely right, he had come here to swindle her, to take her for all he could get. Gerry looked at the front door, and then examined the flap in his hands through its polythene wrapping.

"Ten pounds," he said.

"Ten pounds!" Immediate disbelief. "You must be joking!"

They both looked at each other. Mrs Jones was still chewing. A trace of chocolate had seeped from one corner of her menopausal mouth. Her haggard face did not look outraged, as she clearly meant it to. The lines were slack and there was defeat in her down turned lips. Only her baggy eyes managed some show of defiance. Gerry saw himself suddenly from the outside, not necessarily as she saw him, but just as someone might see him coming into the hallway now. There he was, a short man, not much shy of sixty, in scruffy clothes, slippers, his face unshaven, his hair weighed back with traffic grime, standing alone with an aluminium cat-flap in his hand, on this greasy lino, in this noisome little hallway, in Market Place, in Hampstead Garden Suburb. So it had come to this. Survival meant nothing more nor less than fit the cat-flap. That was his job, his livelihood, his rôle, his meaning, his recognition, the sum and total of it. Everything either proceeded or receded from this point in this hallway, to, from and through the cat-flap.

Ah well.

And he knew what was in his own eyes as he stared back at Mrs Jones. Something far colder and fiercer than the mock indignation which Mrs Jones was trying to summon to hers. He knew that his eyes, right now, were full of a dry and wilful repudiation. He would not do this. If this is what it had come to, if this now was the great challenge of his life, to fit the cat-flap for this person, this grub of humanity, then he would not meet it.

He would kill her. He would kill her and take her bloody money anyway. Or he would turn aside and walk away, still with some vestige of dignity, and do away with himself somehow or other. At last, he believed, he had the courage, the self-respect to do that.

"Here," he said, tossing the cat-flap at her feet. "Fit the fucker yourself."

Mrs Jones said nothing. She had stopped eating a moment, but then, as if to show shock would mean some loss of face, she resumed chewing her Mars Bar.

Gerry turned at the door.

"And good day to you, ma'm!"

Chapter Seventeen

Rumpus

"Has there been a rumpus?"

Gerry's voice was clear on the landing, icy clear and controlled, but inside he felt control slipping away. He felt himself give in, without hesitation, to the viciousness he'd felt in Mrs Jones' corridor, to the viciousness he'd felt when attacking Webb in his bedroom three nights previously, that had left him so drained and spent and hungover. But now it was far, far worse. No hectoring and ranting this time. Rather a slipping and sliding into an act of violence. His eyes darted about the landing for a weapon, a lump of wood, a discarded shoe, anything.

They were clearing him out!

Before he'd reached his landing, before he was even halfway up the stairs, his cardboard box of dirty washing, from his bedroom, *his* bedroom, had been lightly tossed over the banister. His dirty clothes, his shirts, his socks, his underwear, lay scattered in the hallway below. The shopping bag liner from the box had puffed free, a final exhalation of his life here. The person who had tossed down the box had gone back to work without even noticing him on the stairs.

Several figures, Alec Webb and Mik and Kim among them, now emerged from the doorways of his living room and his bedroom.

"Has there been a rumpus?" he repeated. "Has there been a bit of a rumpus?"

No reply.

"Just what do you think you are doing?"

Alec Webb came forward from the bedroom, and with this assumption of responsibility the others shuffled back to their various tasks. Was it Webb himself who'd tossed down his laundry box?

"I think I can explain, Gerry. We're having a spring-clean, you see."

Following Webb's lead, Kim stepped forward, stopping just behind Webb. Her lips were pale with hurt.

"What did you do to my paintings?"

Gerry stared back at her. What paintings? Oh. Those paintings. She looked utterly dismayed, poor child, quite riven with grief and self-pity. Emotion cleaved her heavy brows.

"Your paintings?" Gerry answered. "I know nothing about any paintings."

"Oh yes you do. And where's my milk?" she demanded, taking another step forward, past Webb. Her fresh face was now flushed with anger and defiance.

Gerry rose on his tiptoes, faced her full on:

"Your milk? It's in your lovely tits, dear!"

He sniggered briefly, on his own, on the cold and silent landing. But inside he was aflame, burning with disgust at his own vulgarity. Oh, but he *hated* them all so much! He held them all in such unutterable contempt. He loathed them all. Where was there a weapon - a stick, a shoe, a knife, a gun, a weapon.

Kim retreated to his living room.

In response to Gerry's viciousness Webb took a different tack.

"Gerry, old boy. We had a call from a Mrs Jones of Hampstead Garden Suburb. She wanted to lodge a formal complaint. She said that a dirty, scruffy, smelly old man had entered her home under false pretences, that he had tried to cheat money from her, and that he had been very rude and foul-mouthed. She was really quite upset. We have decided that you answered her description to the letter."

The energy that had briefly suffused Gerry's exhausted body, that had carried him up the stairs on a surge of anger and raised him on his tip-toes, now deserted him. When he spoke his voice was flat and dull and almost uninterested.

"What has that got to do with me?"

Webb stepped forward. In front of members of his Cooperative he could not let such insolence pass.

"You broke into our office, Gerry. You stole our bag of tools. You wrecked our paintings." He looked down a moment at Gerry's tartan feet. Gerry looked down also. "You ripped our order book. You went out and insulted one of our clients. Enough is enough, Mr Delaporte. As far as we are concerned you have made yourself a pretty undesirable citizen here. Persona non grata, if you like. We have decided that we no longer want to live with you and we are clearing out your rooms."

"Are you now?"

"We are indeed!"

Apart from Webb, Mik, hanging back as always, was the only one left in this dramatic confrontation on the landing. The others had begun to resume their labours behind the scenes in Gerry's rooms, beyond the half open doors. Gerry's mattress, stripped and set on its side, was being shunted out of his bedroom behind Webb by invisible hands. The mattress stopped moving and leaned in the doorway. Jake emerged from behind it. He seemed little taller than the width of the mattress.

"Where to?"

He flicked an uneasy glance at Gerry. He was uncertain about all this, it seemed. About clearing Gerry out. About clearing out the dirty, scruffy, smelly old man.

"Downstairs, Jake," Webb said. "For the moment."

Jake went back inside the bedroom and exchanged a few mumbles with a fellow worker. The mattress stayed where it was. They were evidently going to wait until the business outside was concluded. Cigarette smoke wafted from Gerry's bedroom.

"You have no right to do this," Gerry protested. "No legal right to do this to me or to anyone else." It was shameful to abuse him like this, when he was so enfeebled and could not fight back.

"Legal right? You stole our property, Gerry. You wrecked our paintings. You brought our organization into disrepute.You took money for milk and came back empty-handed, then insulted the person who lent you that money in good faith."

Webb could go on like this forever, of course. Mik was still there, hanging back. Gerry thought he detected pity in his dopey expression and he tried to appeal to it.

"I am very tired, Alec, and I need to lie down. I need my mattress, you see."

He glanced sideways at Mik, for whom he'd bought that wine, for whom he'd opened his toilet.

"Mik and Kim are moving down here," Webb announced. "We shall return to our original plans for the upstairs rooms. Office. Interview room. Waiting room. For the time being you can stay on the ground floor. That's until you find somewhere else. But only on one condition."

Gerry did not respond.

Webb looked at him steadily, knowingly. "It's very simple, Gerry, you see. Nothing much at all. You took a bag of our tools, didn't you? We need those tools. We need them to do our work. They were good tools, for good work. Our work. Our work! We need them back. You must go and fetch them. That's all. Go fetch the tools back, Gerry."

Gerry gave a dry and hopeless laugh. "You know I can't do that. You know I can't. Look at me. I only just made it back here."

"But you have no choice, Gerry, old boy. Show willing. Stiff upper lip. Think of it as penance. Put a little iron in your soul, now. Forgiveness must be earned, you know, worked for, like everything else."

"I need to lie down."

Webb stepped forward, resolute.

"And so you may, Gerry. But not until we get our tools back. Then you can rest in peace, I promise."

Chapter Eighteen

Café Society

There had been some total change of perspective. Uphill, approaching Hampstead Garden Suburb, the sky drew down lower, greyer. His thoughts would not retrace their way to the given options. He was aware of some noisy action on the fields, Lyttleton Playing fields, of boys, heavy boys, older boys, running and plunging down the touch-lines with such weight and force he thought he could feel the ground tremble beneath him. An underground train, perhaps. The game, the game! The cut and thrust, the push and shove, the hurly-burly. All still going on. And long may it continue, under these wintry skies, in this cold, drab land. At Aylmer Road the game changed, became more selective, expensive and civilized: he was passing Highgate Golf Course. Now, if some long lost friend or relative were suddenly to wave his sand iron through the undergrowth and cry, "*Gerry! Gerry Delaporte! What the devil's happened to you, old man? Good grief. I remember you. Come on back to the clubhouse and we'll get you cleaned up. We'll find you a set of togs and we'll sit you at the bar with a hot toddy. How's that? Then you can tell us all about it. Not bad bar snacks either, old man - we do ourselves proud here. I'm sure someone'll have a shaving kit. Where's Anna?*"

Perhaps she was over there already, on the Highgate Golf Course, keeping herself fit and in good trim, wearing a member's golf cap, a navy blue golf cap, with embroidered insignia. Perhaps she had spent some of his commuted pension on a life membership. Good for her. She had always wanted to take it up. A social sport. Perhaps he should go and ask after her. You never knew. He could be no surer she was not there than anywhere else. A fifty-fifty chance, then. Not bad odds at all. Worth the gamble. Perhaps he would pop along to the clubhouse and make enquiries - but later, later, later.

He had left behind Highgate Wood, further down the hill. He would remember that. Highgate Wood.

But what was this?

What a stroke of luck! On his side of the road, an old-fashioned trestle board set out on the pavement. On it was chalked, 'Restaurant, 50 yds'. This he needed. He was ravenous. He'd eaten nothing for nearly twenty-four hours, and those twenty-four hours had been the most extraordinary and stressful and well-travelled of his entire fifty-eight years. So he would jolly well sit himself down and have the most glorious meal they could offer. He would drink their best wine. It would be some plonk, no doubt, and he would criticize it, tell them it was over-priced and inferior, from too far north, perhaps, but he'd demand another bottle all the same! He'd abuse everyone in imperious tones in both English and French, with some Italian thrown in for good measure. He'd have a laugh, for goodness' sake, he'd have a laugh! And he'd eat them out of house and home. The chef would be in despair! Thrashing around! And when they presented the bill he would not pay. Not a penny. Can't pay, won't pay. They would call the police and he would have a lift back into London in a warm Volvo and spend a quiet night in the cells somewhere, or in an interview room, lying beneath a clean white Formica table. He'd do the very same thing the following day, but at a more expensive restaurant. Yes, this would be a wonderful way to go. The road of excess leading directly to the palace of wisdom.

It did look a very tatty restaurant, though. There was no sign of any menu outside. There were none of the usual stickers for charge and credit cards. Gerry approached the door, which was let in from the pavement, up a high step, and as he did so the door opened with a jerk and a tall black man stumbled forth from the restaurant. They were in each other's way and their eyes met momentarily. Gerry thought he knew the man from somewhere, from some not so distant meeting. He saw a look in the man's eyes which startled him and which he could not comprehend. There was something stricken about the look, something riven within the eyeball itself. The man hesitated a second then passed by and walked on downhill towards Aylmer Road and Archway Road, in the direction from which Gerry had come. Gerry stared after him a few moments. The gait of the man was wavering and uncertain and shambling, as if he had no idea where he was walking to.

Gerry sighed – *Can't place you, I'm afraid. But good luck! Best of British!* - and stepped up into the restaurant.

It was empty, apart from one table in the far corner, near

the bar area, where an old, white haired man was sitting. He was facing away, towards a wall decorated with unframed Mediterranean scenes, pictures of vineyards and fishing boats, roads lined with poplars, sunny Athenian ruins, all cut from calendars. Gerry cast his eye around the place. The furniture was all mismatched, as if it were the house style. Lots of different kitchen chairs and a motley selection of tables, some of the kind used as pub garden furniture. Beer Garden furniture. Stolen goods, perhaps.

Gerry was aware that from behind the bar he was being critically and cynically examined, but he refused to look back in that direction.

The restaurateur was a heavy-set man in his mid-thirties. His hair was slicked back from flushed and pudgy brows. It was only marginally warmer in the restaurant than it was outside, but he wore a green sports singlet, of the style that gives generous exposure to the armpit. At the end of his bare arm was a tall, slender-waisted glass of blond beer, with creamy head, the kind of drink favoured by the alcoholic still careful of his levels. The glass twisted in his grip, nervous of the lustful fingers at its base. The restaurateur had scowled at his new customer: Gerry was a piece of litter, a sticky wrapper, a scrap of soiled tissue fallen from the walkway railings and blown in from the street.

But now Gerry stepped boldly on and took a seat at a table quite close to the white haired man, thinking that it would be easier somehow to establish himself in the place if he were near this other solitary customer. He sat down and knitted his hands in a steeple and waited to be served. When he had eaten and got his strength back, he told himself, he would press on and get the tools. Sir Alec's tools. Two Strong Arms. T.S.A. in yellow insulation tape. Plenty of time, plenty of time.

A thin woman, infirm and emaciated, emerged from a partition door at the rear, which she quickly closed behind her, cutting off the sound of a lavatory cistern. She looked sheepish, anxious, as if her experience in the lavatory had been disappointing and unpleasant, a nasty secret which she must bear alone. She patted her dark dry perm and smiled as she approached Gerry's table, exposing small and crooked yellow teeth; surprisingly old and glistening yellow teeth. Gerry looked down to the menu, which he had taken from another table. He was surprised to find the restaurant purportedly served middle-eastern cuisine. Kebabs. Koftas. Salads with tomato, feta and shallots. Olives. All this was very appealing.

"Arre yerr rready te orrder, sirr?" she asked. The voice was Scots. Lowlands, perhaps. "All ourr dishes arre the finest Turrkish specialities."

Gerry was about to order a lemony kebab, a double side salad with olives, and ask to see the wine list, when there was an interruption.

"Hold it, Belinda."

It was the restaurateur from behind the bar. He was coming out from there. He approached the table and stepped past Belinda. He set his hands on the back of the beechwood kitchen chair opposite and rested his drunken bulk. He looked as squarely as he could at Gerry, who had the impression from the man's shaky eyes, from his demeanour, from his slovenliness, and from the fumes which poured off him, that he had been drinking since before breakfast.

"We don't serve hoboes, Mister."

Gerry frowned up at him, unafraid, nothing to lose. "Hoboes, sir?" he replied, in his cultured tones. "I should think not."

Belinda looked to her business partner but his sodden

gaze remained fixed on Gerry.

"You're a bum. We don't serve bums."

"I am not a bum, sir," said Gerry, and he laughed. "And may I add that this is the first restaurant I have ever patronised where I have been so greeted. Je ne suis pas un *bum*, Monsieur. Je suis un vrai *gentleman*."

He smiled up at the restaurateur, then looked down and gave his cutlery a brief, nervous inspection. He looked up again:

"Have you such a thing as a napkin?"

The restaurateur sighed, as if he'd dealt with just such a problem a thousand times before, and with his sigh the fumes of this morning's drinking, and last night's drinking, and the fumes of the drinking of the day before which his body had still not processed, all these fumes of the last few days sank about the table in heavy wreaths and layers, and Gerry sat in them, under them, the sinking wreaths and layers, and said nothing.

"So let's see the colour of your money, professor."

Gerry tried to look haughty, incredulous. "I beg your pardon?" He took up the menu and slapped it lightly on the plastic table. But after this gesture he found he had nothing to say, no decent defence. He could only manage a string of clichés. "This is really going too far, sir! What effrontery! To be asked, before I have had a morsel of the delicious fare on offer in your establishment, to be asked to get out my wallet - well, what on earth is going on? It's ridiculous! I shall do my best simply to ignore what you have said and forget all about it. I could very well say something rather offensive, but I shall spare the sensibilities of present company." He nodded to the thin and anxious Belinda, from whom, he noticed, there emanated a slightly faecal scent.

The restaurateur jerked his head towards the door.

"Get out."

Belinda put a restraining hand on the restaurateur's arm. Gerry glanced at her. Might he appeal to her?

"He may fool you, Belinda," said the restaurateur, without taking his eyes off Gerry, "but he doesn't fool moi." He nodded again to the door. "Get out."

Heartened by Belinda's hesitation Gerry turned to the only other person who might exert some favourable influence here. He had realized, as soon as he sat down in this place, that he was literally starving. He did not think he had the energy to take one more step. His legs felt like sticks on the hard kitchen chair. He had burned away any fat in his thighs and buttocks. All this shuffling back and forth, all this toing and froing, all the way from Notting Hill! And he had not eaten a thing since squandering his last pieces of silver in that chocolate machine on the platform at Birmingham New Street, yesterday evening. *But he must not think of that!* Not of Birmingham New Street. Not of that maroon and cream, antique chocolate machine, and the cup of tepid coffee in his hand. Nor of Pwllheli, nor of Bangor, Caernarfon Castle in the mist, nor of Detective Sergeant Aldwich, Aldy, nor of the bearded bobby, nor of the proud and helpful, foolish and deluded, Detective Sergeant Tenmere – Tenpence - whose daughter had recently passed her driving test - No no no! None of them. Not allowed.

Gerry turned to his left, towards the white haired gentleman just three tables away. "I say," he said. "I say there. Perhaps you could arbitrate a moment in our little dispute here, brother. Come and help, eh?" The old head turned a fraction, but no more. There was a cup of tea in one hand and a cigarette burned low in the other. "You may be the last civilized person left in this country, my friend, excluding my good self and this venerable lady here, our charming hostess. Tell me sir, if you would, is it or is it not behaviour unbecoming a gentleman to ask to see a guest's wallet before serving him his food? Is it or is it not behaviour unbecoming a gentleman?"

But the old head turned slowly back.

"Enough of this," the restaurateur said, clearing a chair so he could get round to Gerry. He was going to throw him out.

But Gerry ignored that threat. He still stared after the old man, whose movements had stirred bemusing shades and shapes of memory. Gerry called out to him: "Help me! Old fellow! Help me! Help me!"

The white head turned into profile once more and stopped. There was a feeble juggling of seat position, and then the old man turned right around to face them fully.

When he saw that face straight on Gerry felt a cold, mortal leak of dismay about his heart. Mr Barrington? Len Barrington? There was no longer any sense to the world. There was no sense at all except the sense of his own imminent disintegration. He stared across the café at the ancient, trembling head, at the thickly nicotined moustache, the mouth with its stained pegs in shrunken gums, the watery, uncertain eyes.

The old man frowned, understanding nothing.

A darkness was closing down Gerry's field of vision, eliminating doubt, confusion, all capacity for thought. He heard from somewhere out there a further scraping of chair-legs on the bare wooden floor. Then his own chair was tipped forward and reflexly he set his hands on the table. He felt two powerful forearms lock under his armpits, and his bony frame was forklifted from the chair and set down on its wobbly ankles between the tables. The restaurateur made a drunken swipe for Gerry's wrist that Gerry easily evaded. The man tried again – he wanted to grab his wrist and wrench his arm behind his back and frogmarch him out. He wanted to do that. To taste that power, to feel his helplessness.

"No need." Gerry said. "No need for that."

With what dignity he could muster he crossed the room to the door. The restaurateur was there ahead of him and had opened the door before he could reach for the handle.

Gerry stepped down from the restaurant to the pavement. The door shut behind him. Traffic surged uphill just two paces in front of him. The lights had changed somewhere and the traffic was filling the air with fumes and noise, tousling his filthy hair in its exhaust, overwhelming his senses, leaving nothing visible ahead but the shaking flanks of lorries and vans, their shaking wing mirrors, their shaking exhausts, just the lorries and vans grinding uphill on the first legs of their journeys north to Manchester, Middlesborough, Ipswich or wherever.